Narcissistic Terrorist

Author Shabbir H M Tankiwala

Disclaimer: This book is a fiction work, Names, Characters, Places or Incidents mentioned either are the product of author's own imagination or are used fictitiously, any resemblance to any actual Person or Persons dead or living, events or locales is entirely Coincidence. **Warning** -- the story contains graphic sex, erotic and grotesque violence scenes,

In downtown Kabul city's upscale locality is a plush bungalow in which lives a six member Pashtun family.

The head of the family is **Adil Bangash** who lives with his wife Farida who is a quintessential homemaker and his four children, Adil's elder son name is 'Karmal' who is studying in high school, his second son name is **Fazal Khan Bangash** and Fazal considers himself ineffable hence he doesn't bother going to school, he discontinued academic studies and stopped going to school when he was just 9 years old and now he is good 15 years of age, Adil also has two young daughters Firdoz and Zarine who is the youngest of the four siblings, both his daughters studies in English high school.

Adil has his own business in Kabul, he trades in construction materials Cement and Paints, Adil is a liberal-minded secular person, he is very progressive and firmly believes in gender equality, when Taliban had taken control of Afghanistan in the mid-1990's, Adil with his family had fled to neighbouring Pakistan, to avoid living under stiff religious rule of the radical Islamist Taliban government, he stayed in Lahore for well over 7 years.

Chapter 1

The dawn has broken out, Farida walks inside the room of her second son Fazal, who is fast asleep, Farida draws the curtains of the window, opens the window the strong sunrays hits on the face of Fazal, it's a nature wake up call to Fazal, Farida gives a body jolt to Fazal, he wakes-up rubs sleep out of his eyes, he tells his mother, mom, today is Friday, why did you disturbed my sleep? You should have allowed me to sleep a little longer, Fazal's comments and his lethargic body language makes his mother Farida furious, she yells at Fazal and says you, my inept son, for you every day of the month is either Friday or Sunday, whole day you have nothing better to do other than reading books, watching TV and surfing internet.

Fazal gets up from his bed and stares at his mother, listening to his wife's Farida early morning rant, Adil walks inside the room and asks his wife Farida and his son Fazal, what's the matter? Why are you both mother and son quarrelling? Fazal replies oh daddy, look at mom, she has today, first thing in the morning started her rant discord, Farida tells her husband Adil our son Fazal is useless boy, he simply waste his time, he dropped out of school at tender age, he doesn't get inspired or motivated by his 3 other siblings who are so dedicated towards their academic curriculum, Adil tries to pacify his angry wife, Fazal hugs his father Adil and tells his mother, mamma, you know it well I have learned everything about life even before I stepped into this world, I've learnt the lesson of life in your stomach itself, I damn don't need anyone to teach me, I learn things on my own, I am self-educating, let the time come, I'll prove my mettle to the whole world, just y'all wait and see my dearest mom and dad I am no less then **Isaac Newton**, Farida laugh and queries what you said something Newton, who is this fellow Newton? Fazal says oh mummy you're so duffer let it be you won't know this man Isaac Newton was incredibly intelligent man he was a scientist, Fazal's mother mocks him says, my son you daydream and brag a lot but in reality you're useless.

Farida cools down her temper she hugs her son Fazal and says, stop bragging my child, Adil interrupts and firmly comments No, my wife, my son Fazal is simply not bragging, I know my son is man of substance, Fazal passionately hugs his mother kisses her on her forehead.

Farida says to Fazal, come to the dining room, I'm getting breakfast ready, Fazal response mamma, I want to eat Partha (Bread) with lots of butter and honey spread on it and I want to eat a couple of boiled eggs, Farida kisses Fazal on his forehead and assures him, my naughty son as you wish, ok I am getting breakfast ready for you, Adil reminds Fazal, do you know today is Friday and we both have to go the nearby village to watch our Afghan national sport **'Buzkashi'** game between Uzbeks team and Pashtun team, Fazal replies, oh, yes, Daddy, how can I forget that, we'll go to watch Buzkashi and cheer for our community **Pashtun team,** Adil replies, ok, my son, now quickly freshen up and come to the dining room to have breakfast.

Fazal freshens up, gets ready, he wears traditional Pashtun attire, wears strong fragrance perfume, and steps out of his bedroom and walks towards the living room, Fazal greets his siblings with a loud “As-salamu-alaykum” he gets equally loud response from his siblings “walay-kum-as-salam”, Fazal resolutely loves his youngest sister **Zarine**, Fazal gives a very passionate kiss on both cheeks to his sister Zarine, Fazal and his family assembles at dining table and together enjoy delicious breakfast.

After breakfast Fazal and his dad “Adil” are ready to move out of the house to go to the ground to watch their favourite Afghan national sport Buzkashi game, before leaving the house Fazal requests to his mother to cook his favourite Serkah Pulao and chicken Qorama for lunch, Farida commits yes ok I’ll prepare your choice of food for lunch, Fazal wishes goodbye to his siblings and to his dotting mother and steps out of his house along with his dad “Adil”.

Adil drives the car and reaches a huge ground on the outskirt of Kabul city, where the Buzkashi game between Pashtun and Uzbeks team has already commenced, Adil parks his car in the rugged terrain, few of his friends and acquaintance when they see Adil and his son emerging out of their car, they approaches them and warmly greets them and exchanges pleasantries, one of Adil’s friend Jamil request him to join a group of men enjoying hookah in a makeshift tent outside the ground, Adil obliges to his friend Jamil’s request and walks up to the tent and joins the hookah session while Fazal finds a spot to comfortably sit and watch the Buzkashi game, few moments later Adil too leaves his hookah session with his friends and joins his son Fazal and they both together cheer for their own Pashtun community Buzkashi Team.

After spending little over an hour of watching Buzkashi game, Fazal feels bored and request his father Adil to leave the ground and go for a long drive instead, Adil a caring father never says ‘No’ to his favourite son Fazal, he agrees to Fazal’s request, they both depart from the ground, Fazal has a passion for driving, he says dad, please, may I have keys of the car, I want to take over the wheels, Adil with aplomb hands him the keys of his car, Fazal takes the driver’s seat and his father enters the car from passenger side door of the car.

Fazal drives the car while driving the car along the picturesque Afghan countryside, Adil comments my son, today is Friday and it's our holiday, Fazal nods his head, Adil asks how about enjoying a tipple? Fazal excited his response oh dad, you are genius, sure, lets enjoy our tipple, Adil knows a local bootlegger or to say a discreet booze seller, he guides his son Fazal to the location where there is a motor garage, Fazal drives the car exactly to the place as his dad 'Adil' guides him, once the car reaches the largely dilapidated and disparate garage, Adil gets off from the vehicle and yells "I have come, is there anyone around?" listening to Adil loud voice a man accompanied by a woman supposedly his wife emerges, Adil whispers in that man's ear, please give me four "Cans of chilled beer," the man nods his head, and he signals the lady his wife to bring out four Cans of chilled beer, the woman obliges and goes inside a small room and removes four Cans of beer wraps them in a polythene bag and brings it out and hands it to her husband, who gives it to Adil, and Adil makes payment to the man, Adil thanks the husband and wife for the beer, and enters his car and tells his son Fazal to hit the gas, Fazal drives the car towards a remote isolated location where he and his dear Daddy can sit and enjoy the beer.

Fazal takes the car on the peak of a mountain and stops the car, Fazal tells come dad this is an ideal place for us to comfortably sit and enjoy our drink, Adil agrees, yes, nice pristine environment, so, let us start our beer session, Fazal replies yes sir, let's start and not waste any more time.

Adil opens the polythene bag in which the beer cans are wrapped, Adil opens two Cans, he gives one to his son and keeps another for himself, Fazal and his dad raises the toast, its mid-day, both Adil and Fazal keep sipping beer while conversing wide range of worldly issues.

In between sips of beer Adil thinks and wonders than ask his son Fazal, he comments my son I understand today is a holiday and we are in good holiday mood, when we return back home your mother must have kept delicious food prepared for us, Fazal stretches his hand puts it on his father's shoulder and with smile on his face, says oh Dad, you are my daddy, you've given me birth, you don't need to take my permission before questioning me, tell me, ask me, anything you want to.

Adil smiles and kisses Fazal on his forehead, and starts, he says my son for the past few days one question regarding you keep haunting my mind, Fazal queries what? Adil elaborates look son we are living in a country like "Afghanistan" arguably the most dangerous country on this planet, Fazal nods his head yes I agree with you dad, so, what? Adil explains the uncertain times are becoming even more uncertain, Adil adds my son, I am greatly and gravely concern with regards to you particularly, despite the fact that I understand you are incredibly intelligent, yet so far you haven't proven your mettle, you dropped out of school, citing the reason, that you are more knowledgeable than your school teachers, when we explained this reason of yours to the world, to other people, they all laugh and ridicule us, that's "me and your mom" these people dismissed your remark and said to us that your son is very **cocky** and that he will regret one day, but I didn't and haven't care about the world and have repose faith and confidence in you.

Fazal grins and says each individual person is free to air his/her views and have habit of giving advice to others, the truth is they do not know anything about my perception and my judgement as to how I perceive things, so dad, let us not bother about the people of this world, just leave me on my own, Adil replies yes, but as your father, I have the right to know from you as to, what plans you have for yourself? You are not and never were you ever interested in school college course, nor do you take interest in our family business despite me having requested you to join me and start working with me, but you are noncommittal.

Fazal empties the Can of beer, then opens the second Can of beer, takes few sips, and preaches his dad.

Fazal assertively reveals his thoughts "*challenging the rules is always a good thinking strategy, but that's not all, by not challenging the rules, our mind gets locked into limited thoughts, and we begin to reconcile with the fact that the same approach, method and strategy is ideal for us, and we stop seeing benefits in trying different approach and methods.*"

Fazal adds, my Dad, I firmly believe in myself and in my instinct, please, you, stop worrying about me, I'll think and do what I want to do and what I want to be in life, I will not think what others are thinking and doing and what others think about me.

Adil quickly finishes his beer and says my son Fazal you are a very eccentric young boy, no one in this world can ever understand you, Fazal replies dad, I'll take your words that you've just spoken as a compliment.

Adil laughs and says look my son, even though we are staying in outrageously conservative society yet I as a head of the family have dared to flout every possible rules set by our ever so insular society, Adil adds I am a liberal and secular-minded person to the core, Fazal nods his head and loudly says this is precisely the reason it makes me feel proud to be your son.

Spending well over an hour drinking tipple chatting and conversing both father and son heads back down the hill to their house.

Adil and his son back home, Adil's wife Farida has cooked traditional Afghan food, the lunch of her son Fazal's choice is ready, Fazal gets fresh and as per family rule, on every Fridays, Adil's family avoid eating lunch on dining table instead prefers to sit on the floor and eat their lunch and dinner in a traditional way, big rug is spread on the floor, the female members of the house lay down food, Fazal with his parents and siblings occupies their place around the rug, Fazal's sister Firdoz takes the onus of serving food in every family members plate, Fazal relishes the delicious food his mother has passionately prepared, Fazal enjoys eating chicken Qorama with butter Naan's (traditional bread) mutton Kebabs and Serkah Pulao.

After the lunch is done, Fazal walks inside his room and doze off to afternoon siesta, his mother Farida and sister Firdoz spends most of the afternoon washing plates and rearranging the house, Fazal's brother Karmal goes to the ground close to their house to play cricket match, while father Adil feeling overwhelmingly tired he to doze off to sleep.

Chapter 2

Life's pretty much the same for Fazal, Fazal is a very introvert and reclusive person, he spends most of his time in isolation, he is avid cricket buff, the interest for cricket Fazal developed in Pakistan while staying in Lahore as a refugee, Fazal does pays occasional visit to close by ground to play his favourite sport cricket.

Fazal has recently found a new friend in "**Jason Parker**" who is an American expatriate, Jason's father is USA government's high ranking officer, currently posted in Afghanistan to advise Afghan government plan and manage country's infrastructure development work, Jason house is in same locality close to Fazal's house.

Fazal spends most of his time in the evening conversing with Jason Parker, he takes Jason out of Kabul city to the Afghan countryside on the rocky mountains, they both enjoy cycling, chatting, Fazal also teaches an American Jason to play Cricket, cricket is a strange game for Jason but he starts to enjoy playing cricket in the dusty field.

Jason's mother **Brenda** also likes her son's friendship with ever so proficient Fazal Khan Bangash, Brenda also occasional pays visits to Fazal's house to spend her time with his mother Farida, Farida becomes good acquaintance of Brenda and Brenda likes discussing with Farida lot about afghan culture and also learn few recipes of authentic Afghan food.

.......One Day........, Adil Bangash returns home from his day long work in the evening, as usual, the first thing he does is, he takes his youngest child Zarine in tow and carries his other daughter Firdoz with his hand and makes her sit on his lap, then Adil tells his wife Farida, tomorrow early morning I have to go on a business cum social trip to the city of **Gardez** which is in Paktia province of Afghanistan, Adil adds I have a business deal to complete plus I'm also invited to attend a birthday bash of one of my business associate Wahab Shah, Farida says ok and questions so, for, how many days you'll be away from us? Adil answers maybe 2 days but in case my business deal takes longer than expected time, in that case, I'll have to extend my stay in Gardez by another day or two, Farida holds Adil's hand and passionately comments No, try to complete your deal in two days and come back home to Kabul soon, 4 or 5 days without you will be too much time, you know how much we miss you, Adil laughs Ok my dear wife, I as well intensely miss y'all but all these trips of mine when I have to travel out of Kabul are my business commitments, Farida response ok, my husband please don't worry about us, you concentrate on your work and I hope you trip to Gardez is successful, I'll get your stuff ready and will also prepare tiffin for you tomorrow early morning, Adil compliment his submissive wife excellent, that's like a good wife, Farida reply Thank you, my dotting husband, come now let us all have dinner then we'll go to sleep early today.

After dinner Adil and Farida calls it a night, but Farida libido is high in seductive mood, she undress wipes her vagina with her panty, fondles her bolls, she is craving for sex pleasure and so is Adil, Adil enjoys his marital privilege by indulging in bodily pleasure, Farida a very committed wife ensures her husband is well entertained, flat nude on bed she renders adequate sex and love to Adil who enjoy sex with seductive Farida.

Next day morning, Farida wakes up early, she quickly prepares breakfast and also prepares tiffin for her husband Adil's journey to Gadrez, while eating breakfast Adil casually ask his favourite son Fazal, are you willing to join me on my excursion? Fazal prompt answer oh, No, dad, what will I do with you? after all it's your personal business visit, No, I am not interested, Farida intervenes in the conversation, this boy is a lazy duck he simply wants to stay in close vicinity of home, confine himself in the four wall of this house, Fazal response oh mom, not again, please don't start nagging so early in the morning, Adil tries to pacify both his son and wife, he laughs and says please don't start your acrimonious argument, I was just joking, Fazal says that's like a good Dad, Fazal's mother fumes and walks inside the kitchen and brings out huge tiffin and keeps it on the table and reminds her husband Adil please carry this tiffin with you on your journey.

Adil finishes his breakfast, Adil hugs Fazal and advises him, in my absence the responsibility of this house lies on you, please take care of your siblings and your mother, Fazal firmly assures yes, daddy, you please don't worry at all, Adil satisfied with Fazal's assurance, he tightly hugs and kisses Fazal, Fazal turns around and hug his mother, says I love you mamma, Adil after hugs and kisses to each of his children on emotional note, he loads his car and say goodbye to his family members and sets on his journey to the eastern afghan city of Gadrez in Paktia province.

Chapter 3

Adil Bangash reaches the city of Gadrez, he is accommodated at one of his old friend Razak's house, Adil after taking much needed rest for a couple of hours, gets ready and steps out of his friend's house to complete his business deals, most of the second day of his business trip in Gadrez, Adil spends meeting his business associates and holds marathon discussion sorting out his business plan, finally late afternoon on second day of his visit Adil completes his business related work and now he is free, he has enough spare time to socialize.

Adil has a social commitment of attending his friend's Wahab Shah's birthday bash, early evening, Adil gets ready, wears traditional Pashtun attire and wear a Pashtun "Pagdi" (headgear), he along with his friend and host Razak together goes to the house of their common friend Wahab Shah's.

Wahab Shah a birthday boy is ecstatic to see his friend Adil coming over to his house and joining him to celebrate his birthday party, Wahab perkily walks up to the door of his house, and warmly greets Adil Bangash, Wahab tells Adil I am profoundly happy with you my friend, that you've come to my house to grace the occasion, Adil equally delighted to be among his friends cheerfully replies my friend its always my pleasure to be with warm hearted friend like you.

Adil blend himself among other guests and enjoys the party chatting and puffing hookah, Wahab has ensured that his guests are well entertained hence for few booze aficionado there is a private arrangement to serve them their choice of wine and beer, Adil one among those few wine aficionado enjoys couple of glasses of wine.

Adil Bangash gets an opportunity to spend time with another of his best friend **Salman Hassan** who also apparently likes to enjoy tipple, Salman on his part has most of the evening ever since he has met Adil keeps staring at him and guessing peculiarly,

After intense thinking and wondering, Salman Hassan holds Adil's hand and takes him outside Wahab's house, Adil after a couple of glasses of wine is squiffy, he queries my friend Salman, why have you brought me outside the house? Inside is a nice birthday party in progress, Salman points his finger up towards sky and replies my friend I understand your feelings my apology to disturb you, but since we've met after long time inside the house there's lot of crowd and noise, hence I can't make any personal conversation with you here outside the house in the lawn in the open air, twinkling stars staring at us from sky, I want to sit and talk to you.

Adil smirks and says friend you are weird, but it's fine with me, let us sit and talk, Salman cravingly simply stares at Adil's face and keeps mum, Adil enquires hey, Salman, where are you lost? I am observing your mind is wandering I guess you wanted to talk to me that's why we have briefly disengaged from our friends inside and we are sitting outside the house of our friend Wahab, Salman listens to Adil's comments, and reacts, my friend Adil, I have some plan for you but I am wondering or to say I am bit jittery to disclose my sly motive behind why I've pulled you out from the party and have requested you to spend some time of yours in private with me.

Adil response you said sly motive very intriguing seems you've some plan for me, but you know my nature very well, I am a simple man and I have no grudge for anyone, tell me, what you have in mind? I promise you, I won't feel bad for anything you tell me or ask me, Salman response oh, really, Adil confirms yes.

Salman begins conversation by saying I know you are a dedicated family man, Adil smiles, Salman ask Adil do you like to have extra curricula fun as well in life? Adil retorts, as in, Salman explains as in, I mean like bodily pleasure fun sex after all you are a wealthy businessman, Adil replies look my friend as I have given you my word of commitment, that, whatever you ask me, I won't feel bad, but I guess you are exceeding your limit, Salman nods his head in disagreement and asseverate my friend, I know it very well you are sincere family man, Salman add, my intentions are humble, but I desperately need your help and only you can help me.

Adil states his mind, No, ifs, No, buts, straight to the point, tell me, what do you expect out of me? Salman assertively response my friend I want you to marry a girl who is hard-pressed, living a sordid life, and our religion permits Man to marry multiple time even while we are married, Adil retorts, Salman my friend, are you crazy, do you know, what you just said or suggested to me? You advised me polygamy, but, why? Salman explains as you know I am 49 year old man, Adil says ok, so, what? Salman elaborates, there is a girl whose name is **Yalda Sultana**, this girl Yalda is my best childhood friend's only daughter, my friend's name was Rameez khan, my friend Rameez and his wife "Yalda's" mother lost their lives during the war between the USA and Islamist Taliban terror army, in a bomb blast both husband and wife were killed, leaving behind two children Yalda and her elder brother orphaned.

Adil empathize ok sorry to listen about this harrowing tragic incident, but, what is it to do with me, Salman says, Yalda's elder brother has deserted her and he has got married and lives with his wife in Pakistan city of Karachi, Adil nods his head, Salman adds this girl Yalda had got married when she was sixteen years old, the boy was from this town Gardez itself, Adil listens and acknowledges. Salman continue saying this boy proved to be a monster, he was a drug addict and to meet his expenses towards his addiction to buy drugs he exploited beleaguered Yalda took away all her valuables and he and his callous father use to ferociously beat Yalda, they also took full possession of her ancestral house and sold it, when all was over, the boy divorced Yalda and mercilessly kicked this young girl Yalda out of his life and out of his house.

Nowadays this young girl Yalda stays at the mercy of one of her maternal aunt, in her aunt's house at their mercy, she's a hapless young girl and desperately needs support of a caring man, Salman proves his point says Adil in you, I find all the right attributes you are the perfect trustworthy man who can give this beleaguered woman much needed help and support, and I assure and promise you she won't let you and your family down, intimately with sheepish expression, Salman says, this young woman Yslda is sexy beautiful, and take my words, she will give you excellent intimate sex fun, a sex that you will enjoy. .

Adil patiently with eyes wide open listened to his friend Salman rhetoric, Adil ask, by the way, if I may ask you, how old is this girl Yalda, what's her age? And, why are you so concerned about her life? Salman replies you've asked a valid question, her age is 19 years and why I am so interested and why am I so concerned about "Yalda" is, simply because she is my dearest childhood friend's orphaned daughter and on humanitarian ground the onus is on me to help my friend's daughter apparently she's like my daughter as well.

Adil reacts, ok, my thoughts are with Yalda my heart goes out for her, listening about her life story the pain and agony she's suffered at such a young age, but, I want to question your wisdom, why me? I am a married man and there is a generation gap between me and Yalda, Adil adds my age is 40 years, and I am a father of 4 children.

Salman tries to convince reluctant Adil, he argues look age is mere numbers, it doesn't matter, trust me, Yalda will serve your purpose, she will prove to be a submissive wife, I assure you for that, she will adjust herself to the situation and blend well within your family, and I'm sure even your wife "Farida" won't object, Salman with folded hands, pleads, please my friend relent and agree to my request, please marry and accept Yalda in your life as your wife.

After intense and exemplary discussion and persuasion by Salman Hassan, Adil Bangash cave-in and agrees to make, Salman friend's daughter "Yalda Sultana" his second wife, Adil gives his consent to Salman that he is willing to marry Yalda, that brings cheers on the face of Salman Hassan.

Salman tells Adil, tomorrow itself I and my wife will make arrangement for you to get married to Yalda, we'll organise your Nikah ceremony at my house, is that, ok, Adil hugs Salman and says, yes, its ok with me friend, Salman replies, Thank you, I will eternally be grateful to you.

Adil and Salman walks back inside their friend's "Wahab's" house and joins the party relishes delicious Afghan delicacies, the party gets over and Adil intoxicated nearly dozen odd glasses of wine and beer, in high spirit he along with his friend Razak returns back to Razak's home.

Next Day, Adil even though reluctantly but on compassionate ground gets ready to become groom for the second time, with mounting concern worried about how his first wife Farida and his four children particularly his intrepid son "Fazal Khan Bangash" will react, but for the time being, Adil galvanise himself and goes to his friend's Salman Hassan's house to attend his own Nikah ceremony (Wedding Ritual).

Salman Hassan and his wife Aneesa plays the role of bride to be "Yalda's" parents, rolling on in fast pace they organised the Nikah Ceremony (wedding Ritual), Yalda all ready to exchange her wedding vow with Adil Bangash.

The Kazi (priest) completes the formality and solemnize Yalda Sultana marriage with Kabul based businessman "Adil Bangash."

The room has been arranged by Salman Hassan for Adil and Yalda to spend their memorable bridal night.

Yalda looking absolutely devastating exceptionally beautiful, donning gorgeous silky Red clothes, Yalda encounters her better half Adil for the first time in private in the room on the bed, feeling sheepish.

Yalda folds her hand and bents on her knees and passionately "Thanks" Adil for accepting her in his life, Yalda promises her unflinching support to her new husband Adil Bangash, Adil becomes emotional he embrace her, says, Thank you, for coming into my life, Yalda assures, I'll give unprecedented respect and affection to your first wife.

Adil request Yalda, tells her, my love this is our bridal night and I'm craving to consummate you, are you ready, Yalda response, is, yes, my dearest, honey my sex drive is running high as well, I too am craving to have sex with you, my vagina is eager to be consummated by you, please go ahead, I'm ready, Yaldaa unravels herself, takes off her clothes, undressed removes her panty and bra, displays her bolls to her new husband, Adil and Yalda cordially and passionately indulges and celebrates there bridal night.

The dawn breaks out, Adil's bridal night with his newly "Wed" wife "Yalda" is over, now, it's time for Adil to head back home with Yalda by his side, Adil and Yalda prepares to leave for Kabul, few of their common friends and relatives come to meet the newly Wed-Couple, the friends and relatives convey to Adil Bangash and his wife "Yalda" their best wishes and bless the couple, Adil loads up his and Yalda's luggage in his car, Yalda gets inside Adil's car and they get genial sent off from their friends, Adil hits the gas and starts his journey to his hometown Kabul.

Chapter 4

On the way to Kabul with mounting horror Adil vividly thinks, as to, what may be the outcome at my home? Will my family accept my second wife? Adil decides, sagacious handling of affair would avoid outright confrontation, he advises his wannabe "Yalda" to exercise maximum Restrain in case his first wife reacts outrageously over his decision to marry her, Yalda assures Adil, there won't arise such a situation and everything will go of smoothly, Adil says, Thank you.

The journey comes to an end, Adil's car reaches his home, Adil's daughter "Firdoz" is the first to spot the car entering the home premises, Firdoz gets excited to see her father arrive, but she is also surprised to see him come home with a beautiful young lady donning a green outfit glaring colour sitting next to her father on the front seat of the car.

Firdoz runs towards her brother Fazal, she hugs him and says, brother our Dad has returned home, Fazal with smile on his face responses, wow, that's a nice news you gave me, Firdoz whispers in Fazal's ear, says, Dad has come back home but he is not alone there a beautiful woman accompanying our Dad, Fazal nods his head, and as he turns around and sees, his Dad "Adil" is standing behind him and behind him is standing his new wife "Yalda," as a gesture Fazal gets up from his chair, Fazal orders his sister to inform his mother "Farida" that Dad has arrived.

Fazal wishes his father As-Salamu-Alaykhum, Fazal stares at Yalda and greets her and ask his father "Adil", Daddy, who is this young woman? Adil feeling sheepish ignores Fazal's query.

Farida emerges out of the kitchen with her youngest daughter in tow, with beaming smile, Farida acknowledges the presence of Yalda, she ask her husband, how are you? Hope your journey to Gardez was successful? And, who is this young girl who's come with you? Adil listening to volley of questions from his wife, reacts, he smatters, than looks at his elder son "Karmal," Yalda standing in the corner keeps silence simply observes the scenario being played out from distance.

Adil walks close to his first wife "Farida" puts his hand on her head, he kisses his younger daughter "Zarine" on both her cheeks than gathers courage and says, Her name is Yalda Sultana, she is from Gardez city and now on she'll stay with us in our house, Farida shockingly gaze into the eyes of her husband, Karmal intervenes, Dad, ok, but, may we all know, as to, why? This woman will be staying in our house, Adil feels shy, he tilts his head down, then, he glances at both his wives top to bottom, than he says, "Yalda" is my wife, we have got married day before yesterday in Gadrez.

Listening to her husband's comments, Farida gets spaced out, her two daughters are too young to understand what's going on, both Firdoz and Zarine holds there mother's fingers and biting their lips observes the proceeding, Fazal gets furious, he says, Dad, ridiculous, this was not expected from you, his elder brother Karmal reaction is more guarded, he smiles and walks inside his room so does Fazal.

Farida is completely lost, she's spaced out, than, Yalda slowly walks towards Farida her senior co-wife now, Yalda can't hold back her tears, she apologies to Farida, she says, my sister, please pardon us, if your feeling have got hurt, I am thankful, to your husband to our husband who have shown great generosity by marrying beleaguered woman like me, Yalda pleads, please accept me, I'm an orphan, and I assure you, that, I am accommodative will adjust myself well with you and your children please make me part of your family, I beg of you.

Yalda's emotional rhetoric pacifies her, Farida hugs Yalda wipes her tears from her eyes and kisses her on both her cheeks and accepts Yalda as her co-wife.

Adil thanks his first wife for accepting his second wife "Yalda" and explains to her, he says, I took the decision of marrying her under distinctly bizarre circumstances, Farida replies, its, ok. We'll all live happily together, Farida's daughters Firdoz and Zarine strikes instant chord with their step mother, Yalda takes both Zarine and Firdoz in her tow and starts conversing with them.

Farida walks inside her son "Fazal's" room, who is lying on the bed in disgust, unhappy that his father has betrayed them by marrying a girl nearly 20 years junior to him. Farida approaches her son "Fazal" and he throws a tantrum, he says, mamma I am profoundly disgusted, how can we accept another woman in our house, Farida tries to convince him, she says, what had to happen has happen, I have accepted her as my "co-wife," and now I want you to for my sake accept that beautiful young girl "Yalda" as your stepmother, Fazal sarcastically laughs, oh, my stepmother, so, now, I'll have two mothers, Farida advises, please come out in the living room and greet your Dad's new wife, Fazal replies, ok, mamma, you're really great, you've big heart, for your sake I'll give respect to my Dad's second wife, Farida Thanks her son for obeying her.

Fazal and his elder brother fall in line and accept Yalda as there stepmother, Fazal graciously approaches his father hugs him and apologies to him for his abrupt behaviour than approaches his stepmother Yalda and greets her with "As-Salamu-Alaykum" and Yalda in turn graciously replies "Walay-kum-As-Salam".

Farida wants to celebrate the occasion, she prepares special meal for dinner, Yalda request Farida to allow her to cook and also to prove her culinary skills,

Yalda realizes how important a person Fazal is in the house, hence it's very important to keep maverick "Fazal" in good humour, Yalda inquires in front of his mother "Farida" with Fazal, she ask him, tell me, what is it that you would like to eat? What is your favourite food? Fazal stares at Yalda and his mother than replies, today I am in a mood to eat Seekh Kebab (Lamb grill Kebab) and Puloa, Yalda ask Fazal, how about me preparing for y'all Narenj Puloa, Fazal excited, oh, really, you know how to prepare Narenj Pulao that's my favourite, Yalda smiles and says, yes, I will prepare Narenj Pulao, Fazal says, excellent, also cook Qorama Lawand, Yalda confirms, yes, you'll get all the food of your choice ready.

Yalda assisted by her senior co-wife "Farida" desirously prepares food for dinner, later, late evening, it's time for the family to enjoy there dinner, the rug is spread, all the family members sits in circle, the plates are laid, Fazal's younger sister "Firdoz" as per Afghan tradition carries the "Aftabah Wa Lagan" (a copper basin, to wash hands), Yalda takes the onus of serving the food, she serves generous quantity of Seekh Kebab (lamb grill kebab) to Fazal who eats kebab with butter Naan (bread), the family thoroughly enjoys the delicious food.

The life goes on tremendously well for Adil Bangash family, Yalda and Farida the co-wives of Adil jell well with each other, Farida's daughters Firdoz and Zarine in particular are very happy with arrival of charming "Yalda" in their family life, Adil on his part balance his marital commitments rather well, he ensures that both his wives are satisfied with him in every aspect.

Almost four months have passed since Adil married and brought Yalda home, one night while Adil is away from home has gone to Pakistan port city of Karachi to book consignment of Cement for his business deals.

It is late evening, after dinner, Fazal is sitting on the sofa reading book, his mother Farida approaches him with washed clothes in her hand, and says, my son, Fazal looks up at his mother and ask, yes, mamma, what is it? Farida replies, I want you to help me, Fazal nods his head, yes, sure, tell me, what? Farida flaunts neatly folded clothes and says, these are the washed clothes of your stepmother "Yalda", she has just gone up to her room few minutes ago and it is not very late, she must be awake please go upstairs to her room and give it to her, Fazal smiles and nods his head, takes clothes in his hand, says, ok, mamma, I'll give these clothes to Yalda and then I to will go to my room and sleep, Farida responses, yes, you go to sleep and I myself to will go to sleep early today as I am very tired, Fazal says, ok, mamma, you go and sleep and I'm going upstairs to give her the washed clothes, Farida says, god bless you my son, thank you.

Farida walks inside her room undress itches her pussy, takes pillow and tightly hugs it presses hard to her protruding bosom, thinks of sex, than, she wears nighty and sleeps with her two daughters, and Fazal is walking step by step upstairs towards the room of his sexy stepmother.

Fazal reaches upstairs encumbered with clothes in his hands, he sees the door of Yalda's room is open and just the curtain covering the entrance of the room, with mounting concern Fazal pushes the curtain on side and he enters the room of his young beautiful gorgeous looking stepmother his Dad is away on business trip and Yalda is alone in the room.

Gosh, what happen? Fazal is standing inside Yalda's room his eyes pops out he is spaced out, why? He is stunned, sees, that Yalda is standing in front of the big mirror without any clothes on her body, **she's nude,** and Yalda is admiring her looks in the mirror, and her soft fleshy sexy ass is staring at Fazal, she is frivolously enjoying her private moments, and not realizing that a young handsome Pashtun hunk is standing and observing her nudity, Yalda swirls and whirls and croons, she rubs her breasts nipples and vagina on mirror to get cool sensation, she is swoon by herself lost in her thoughts, and so is Fazal khan Bangash swoon and completely lost in his own world, Fazal quietly stands and enjoys seeing his stepmother nudity and sex.

Suddenly, Yalda spots a shadow and she turns back sees its her stepson "Fazal" standing and observing her intimate nude activities, she takes long strides towards her bed and pulls the chador and covers herself, she is furious and confused, she says, hey you, boy, how come you are here in my room at this time of the day at night? Fazal flabbergast sexually aroused, he smatter, he is at loss of words.

Yalda queries, when did you entered in my room? aren't you suppose to knock the door before entering someone's room, that too, in the room of a young beautiful lady, Fazal replies, I'm sorry, I'd come to give you your clothes which my mother had given to me to give you, Yalda continues her tirade, you are my stepson, aren't you aware, I am your stepmother and your father is away on business trip, don't you know that whether its girls of boys everyone likes to enjoy their private moments, I am a nineteen year old girl and I have lust for intimacy, my longings for sex and intimate pleasure, Fazal racks his brain, what to do, but, I am enjoying the situation.

Fazal response, I am extremely sorry, I won't do it again, Yalda reacts, what do you mean? By saying, won't do it again, why you did it today? Fazal replies, I am sorry again take these clothes of yours and I'm going downstairs to my room, Fazal turns his back as he is above to step out of the room, Yalda yelps, hey, you young boy, Fazal ask, yes, what? Yalda says, now, where are you going? Fazal replies, to my room to go to sleep, Yalda cravingly responses, you'll go away from my room, you'll go living me alone in my room, you don't have shame, you'll live young woman alone, Fazal thoroughly obfuscate by Yalda's reaction, says, yes, I have to go to my room, Yalda adds, you've just seen me nude, Fazal with mounting horror gaze at Yalda's face, Fazal apologizes, sorry my mistake, Yalda responses, so, what mistake? Mistakes happens, we human do make errors.

Yalda inquires, do you have a girlfriend? Fazal replies, No, Yalda ask, oh, why' No? you are a hunk, Yalda queries, have you ever before seen a woman without clothes before, Fazal confuse, smatters, Fazal thinks of his mother because he often sees his mother **nude without clothes**, and sometimes his mother disrobe flaunts bolls and vagina gives him intimate tight sexy hugs and kisses, Farida age in her late thirties equally sexy with intense sex appeal, but in front of Yalda, Fazal is baffled, he hesitates, Yes than No, again Yes than No, Yalda says, stop muttering Yes, No, Yes, No, give me precise answer, have you ever seen a woman nude before? Fazal assertively says, yes, Yalda reacts, oh, my goodness, you boy have seen a woman Nude, this is not what I expected of you, I thought you are a humble young man.

Fazal shrugs of thoughts of his mother nudity, he takes couple of steps forward moves close to Yalda looks straight in eyes of Yalda, and replies yes, about four years ago, there was a woman whose husband use to work on ship, while her husband was away once I happen to go to her house as my friends use to stay in her neighbourhood, hence once she called me in her house and seduced me, and we had sex.

Yalda breathes heavily and says, you creep, so, you've had sex before, Fazal nods his head in agreement, confidently answer, yes I have, Yalda again ask, but, you are otherwise very intelligent boy, than, why did you entered my room without knocking the door? Fazal sufficiently arouse, replies, ***Beauty opens the door but only Virtue enters***.

Yalda listens to what Fazal just said and she passionately ask, will you sleep in my room with me today? I am your father's wife and I happen to be your stepmother, you saw me nude, is it ethical for us to sleep in nude together on same bed and is it ok to for us to copulate? We both are young and at this moment we both have extreme high lust for sex, Fazal says, darling love, you have such wonderful ass and sexy juicy fat bolls (breasts), this is not a moment to think of ethics, incest, Yalda understands, she drops the chador that she has draped to cover her body, Fazal glances at Yalda scintillating body top to bottom and bottom to top, enough passion has arouse, and both Yalda and Fazal can't control there longings, Fazal hugs nude Yalda admire her body, and profoundly kisses her all over her sexy body.

Fazal and Yalda both young and desperate frivolously indulges in sexual pleasure, all night experiencing wild fantasy, the night passes on, and Yalda's and Fazal's passion gets enhance, both enjoy there pleasure.

The night is over, the dawn breaks out, Fazal's mother "Farida" wakes up, she knows that Fazal is a late riser as he doesn't go to school or work, she's surprise to notice that her co-wife Yalda is still not emerged out of her room, the time is 8.00 am, Farida enquires with her elder son about Fazal's whereabouts, Karmal replies, he's not aware, Farida gets her children ready and sends them to school.

Around 8.30 am, Farida decides to walk upstairs to her co-wife "Yalda's" room, oh look what happen the door of Yalda's room was left open yet again, Farida enters the room, and to her dismay, she sees, the horrific scene that she couldn't have imagined in worse of her nightmare, she spots the apparent, Farida sees, her favourite son "Fazal" and her husband's young love Miss Yalda Sultana are sleeping in compromising condition.

Farida in shame and disgust cups her hands and holds her face, and says, shame on y'all, she gives a body jolt to Yalda, Farida shouts, y'all shameless please wake up its morning, Yalda wakes, shouts, oh my god, what happen? Farida turns her back and stands in opposite direction as she unhappy disgust to see her son in inappropriate physical condition, Farida with her back to Yalda and Fazal, says, my shameless family members, y'all with this disgrace act have smirch the family's reputation, Fazal wakes up, Yalda frowns looks at Fazal and Fazal looks back at her.

Farida goes away from the room walks downstairs, Yalda ask Fazal, my dear, your mother reaction is fierce and furious as expected, what will happen? Fazal replies, chill, don't worry, I'm with you, Yalda starts crying, she says, what will happen if your father who's my husband comes to know about us spending night together on same bed? Fazal once again assures, don't worry, nothing to fear, we've just had pleasure, incest is too common in Muslims households, Yalda responses, ok, I'm taking your words, it's your responsibility now to protect me from any apparent danger, Fazal kisses Yalds on her checks and breasts then confidently reiterates, done, I'll protect you.

Yalda and Fazal get up from bed with mix feelings of overnight pleasure and concerns with regards to what may happen how their family members would react, after discovering immoral chemistry between them, Yalda and Fazal freshens up, Yalda before walking downstairs in the living room of the house with passion whispers in the ears of her allege paramour and her stepson "Fazal," she says, you were fantastic on bed, I thoroughly enjoyed the **intimate Dash** with you honey, Fazal reacts, by kissing Yalda, than says, come be prepare to face the music, my mother and your co-wife will rant her anger.

Farida sitting on the sofa of the living room, eagerly waits for her son and her co-wife to appear before her.

Yalda and Fazal with mounting unease together enters the living room, Farida overwhelmingly upset after witnessing the disgrace behaviour of Fazal and Yalda, as soon as she spots them, she gets up from sofa register a tight slap to her son "Fazal" than she grumbles and gives a severe "dressing down" to Yalda, she tells her co-wife "Yalda" you promiscuous woman, you've broken the trust of our sincere husband "Adil" you've smirch the husband wife relationship by indulging sexually with your own young stepson.

Yalda emotional drama, she breaks down emotionally listen to the rant of her senior co-wife, she weeps and says, oh, my dear, you are like my elder sister, please forgive me please forgive us, both I and Fazal are young, and we just failed to control our longings, Yalda adds, you know it, in young age, the desperation is high and always crave for pleasure.

Fazal quietly standing and listening the discord between his allege paramour cum stepmother and his real mother, Fazal steps into conversation and says to his mother, oh, mamma, come on, have a big heart, please pardon "Yalda and me, Farida replies, oh, No, my naughty son, I can't pardon you for your vices.

Fazal comments, Great Virtues as well as Great Vices makes a Man Great.

Fazal tells Yalda to move out of the room for few moment as he wants to talk something personal to his mother, Yalda says, ok, and she goes out of the room, leaving the mother and son alone in room,

Fazal than comes close to his mother, put his arm around her waist, lifts the gown that his mother is wearing, finds that his mother is not wearing undergarment no panty, he spanks his mother's ass, gives a mouth locked lip kiss, say mom where is your panty, you wearing no bra and panty, Farida simply smiles, says, I want to give my vagina fresh air to breathe, Fazal holds his mother (Farida) body tight and kisses his mother on her bolls, Farida tells her son, you naughty fellow be careful someone will see us mother and son indulging in intimate intimacy, control your longings and lust, Fazal says, mom, you as well are young hot sexy, you as well have crush on me, we two as well indulge in intimacy have body pleasure often when we are alone at home, you do make me kiss your breasts, you do also flaunt your nudity to me, mamma same thing happen, yesterday night when I went upstairs to Yalda's room, she was alone and was nude and was entertaining herself. Farida says, okay enough now you don't have to narrate anything more, because I know you entered her room and both of you vulnerable, took advantage of situation and seduce each other and indulged in sex, Fazal says, wow, smart girl, and Fazal kisses his mother all over, in turn Farida as well kisses her son Fazal.

Farida now happy herself in intimate mood, she whispers in her son Fazal's ear, now let us call that stupid girl bitch Yalda inside the room, Farida arranges her hair, adjust her dress, wipes her face, then, she yells Yalda's name call her inside, she relents and says, ok, stop this drama, I pardon you both for the immoral activity, Farida kisses her co-wife "Yalda" on both her cheeks and says, better be careful next time, Yalda responses, you are great.

Yalda runs upstairs on the terrace of the house, she sits on the floor of the terrace, and feeling ashamed she covers her face with both her hands, seeing Yalda running upstairs on the terrace, Fazal follows her as well, Fazal spots Yalda sitting on the floor in the shade, with her hands covering her face, Fazal puts his hand on Yalda's head and ask, what's the matter? What are you pondering about?

Yalda replies, my dear, I wished if I were to have controlled my feelings last night, Fazal replies, how was it possible? we both were sexually aroused and were desperate for fun, I saw you nude and you were happy to saw me your nudity, Yalda comments, what a dichotomy in my life, Fazal queries, what dichotomy you are talking about, Yalda answers, than, what, this is a bizarre dichotomy, I have fallen in love with two men now and the dichotomy is the both men's whom I love are by relation father and son, my love with father is official while love with son is, "Yalda pause", Fazal prompts her, why did you stop? Please complete your sentence, Yalda says to Fazal, No, you'll feel bad if I say more, Fazal laughs, No, how can I feel bad, you say anything you like, I'll listen, Yalda completes her sentence, she says, my love with father is legal and son is illegitimate, Fazal laughs and says, oh, this is what you mean, never mind I and my father are modern folks, we hate and reject stupid foolish Islam, we are liberal and secular, such relationship won't make any significant difference, Fazal brags, says, my father is wonderful man, he is modern and progressive.

Chapter 5

The life goes on for Adil Bangash and his family.

FOUR YEARS HAVE PASSED, since the time Adil had married for the second time to a girl from Gadrez Miss Yalda Sultana, these four years have been full of bliss for Adil's family, Adil's family has become a quintessential happy family, the people of Kabul compliments Adil for successfully managing to keep his fairly large family united and happy, particularly succeeding in balancing his Marital responsibility between his two wives, Adil keeps both his wives "Farida and Yalda" happy and entertained.

Adil's second son the ineffable "**Fazal khan Bangash**" though initially reluctant but has now started working with his father and helps him or rather he himself has taken over the responsibility of running his father's trading business,

Also in the past four years the stork has once visited Adil's second wife Yalda, Adil's fifth child and Yalda's first, Yalda has given birth to a "Baby Girl" and has named her "Heena".

Just when Adil Bangash was enjoying the most propitious moment of his life.

Gosh a tragedy struck, Adil Bangash had gone to Pakistan city of "Peshawar" to attend his friend's son wedding reception, he had gone alone, and a rather unfortunate event happened, while Adil was having his lunch in one of the roadside restaurant in a crowded area, a terrorist detonated a bomb, it was a suicide terror attack, the explosion of the bomb devastated the whole area killing dozens of innocent people, but sad part is that among many victims "Adil Bangash" also became a victim.

Adil died on the spot, when the news of Adil's death reached his home, the whole family particularly both his wives "Farida and Yalda" were shattered and inconsolable.

Fazal accompanied by his elder brother Karmal rushed to Pakistan city of "Peshawar" to perform the last rites of their father.

Chapter 6

Few weeks have passed since the dead of the head of the family Adil Bangash, as his elder brother Karmal stays in Pakistan city of "Lahore" where he has gone for further higher studies, and he has no interest whatsoever in family business, hence the onus is now on Fazal's shoulder to look after the family members and family business and financial responsibilities.

Fazal takes care of both his family business and family, Fazal finds it increasingly difficult to console his three younger sister "Firdoz, Zarine and stepsister Heena" all his three sisters profoundly miss their father.

Fazal and his now widowed stepmother Yalda have special feeling and liking for each other, gradually there chemistry has evolved.

One day late afternoon while Yalda is sitting along with her co-wife "Farida" with her own daughter Heena recumbent on her lap, Fazal returns home early from his work.

Fazal gets fresh, Yalda serves Fazal a glass of juice and snacks, Fazal after eating snacks and finishing drinking juice, he sits close to his mother and tells her, mamma, today I've something special to talk to you, Farida nods her head, yes, tell me, what? Yalda sitting opposite to Fazal as well stares at Fazal's face with curiosity to listen what's so special he is above to say.

Fazal stands up moves close to Yalda, he passionately holds her hand, and gives assertive affectionate kiss to Yalda staright on her bolls, Yalda feels sheepish and also surprised with Fazal attitude, Fazal's mother "Farida" stunned to see her son holding the hand of his widowed stepmother "Yalda".

Fazal says, mamma, I resolutely love this woman "Yalda" and I want to marry her, Yalda thoroughly surprise and flabbergast, she's happy as well she can't control her emotion.

Fazal's mother questions his wisdom, she says, my son, how is it possible, this woman "Yalda" is a widow of your father and how will it be possible for me from being her senior co-wife, how will I make her or accept her as my daughter-in-law?

Fazal shrugs off his mother's concern, instead he ask Yalda, do you love me? Are you ready to become my better half? Ready to marry me?

Yalda smirks she stares at both Fazal and his mother "Farida", she hugs and kisses Fazal's mother takes her daughter in her tow and nods her head, says, yes, if your mother allows, I'm ready to marry you, Yalda jokingly laughs and says, as it is we both have been indulging in intimate sex acts, let us make our sex legal, so that I can legally sleep nude with you without any fear, and Yalda walks away from the room.

Fazal sits close to his mother kisses her on her breasts, Farida tells, my son let us go inside bedroom, I want to have important discussion with you, Fazal says okay lets go in and talk private matter in private, Fazal holds his mother's hand and walk inside bedroom, Fazal stares all over the house sees no one close to the bedroom, Fazal quickly walks inside the kitchen opens refrigerator and removes couple of Beer and walks back to his mother's bedroom, Fazal closes door of the room ensure windows are closed, makes the room settings darker, Farida unravels removes her clothes just leave the panty on her body, Farida lies on bed, Fazal removes his shirt, and sleep on his mother sexy body, Farida now is in her Forties but still a young widow, lust for sex.

Farida questions Fazal, she ask, my darling son you are handsome young man, this woman Yalda is divorcee from her first husband, then she married your father and now as Adil my believed husband is death, she (Yalda) is widow, Yalda is heavily sexed smirch woman, Farida further continues saying, Yalda is known promiscuous woman, she indulged in sex with you and you are her stepson.

Farida removes her panty and says, my sex darling I want fun, please give me bottle of chilled Beer, Fazal obliges take my sexy mom enjoy chilled beer, Farida takes couple of sips of beer and softly make request, darling son Fazal give me a sexy kiss on my vagina, Fazal obliges, oh sure mom with pleasure I will, he licks his mother fancy tight pussy, Farida pleasantly enjoy her son licking and kissing her cunt and gently pressing her breasts kissing her nipples, Farida finishes her beer and she says thank you darling, your kisses are so fantastic and sweet, Fazal happy, he gives a lip tight kiss to his mother, now, Farida says, my sweetheart son, please reconsider your decision, you can continue your intimate relationship with Yalda, you can continue to fuck her copulate, but you better marry a young girl from dignified family background. Fazal takes a deep breathe, open a Can of beer, drinks entire beer in one shot, Farida craving for sex pleasure, now she is full nude, Fazal says, wow, mom, you so sweet and sexy, let me give you a fuck, Fazal removes his pants, and suck his dick in his mother pussy.

Fazal gets up from bed, drinks another beer, Fazal philosophically says, my darling mother, Islam is horrible shit religion, in fact Islam is not religion Islam is madness, Farida says, as a child in my parent house we used to practise Islam, but once I got married to your daddy, Adil used to hate Islam and for valid reason, therefore our family is liberal and secular despite the fact we living in country which full of religious fanatics idiots, Fazal says, lucky we are that our daddy guided us in right direction.

Fazal says, in Islam the Muslims men marry girls their bride is/are decades younger to them, Muslims men marry female who is their granddaughter's age, a sixty year old Muslim man marry a girl who is just sixteen or eighteen year old, and this Muslim man or men have weak **peni dick** no energy to perform sex, cannot satisfy their teenage wives, so, obviously these unfortunate Muslim brides who are so young with high sex drive, need someone to satisfy them, so, these Muslim girls compel to adopt promiscuity, take for example Yalda there was age difference of 20 years between daddy and Yalda, now daddy is death, and this woman Yalda in her mid-twenties, obviously young Muslim widows need intimate pleasure, Farida says, you know what my son, even your daddy was aware of your intimate relation with Yalda, but he applied a stoic silence and ignored it, Fazal laughs and says yes, I know it. Farida spreads her legs itches her vagina, she says, darling give me one more fuck and then we move out of this room, Farida says, you can understand my situation as well, I am so hot sexy babe, your father though we produced four kids, but, your father was not particularly good in bed, that's why I found a sex in my own son, it is you (Fazal) who satisfy me, also that poor Yalda find sex pleasure with you, let me "matter of fact" tell you your father did not satisfied Yalda, Yalda loves having sex with you, Fazal fondles his mother breasts licks her vagina, Fazal suck his dick in Farida's pussy.

Farida over joyed gulps second bottle of beer and indulge herself "**blow job**," Farida gives oral sex to his son Fazal, and Fazal is happy, Farida says, my darling I thoroughly enjoy sex with you, and I give you my consent to go ahead and marry your father's widow promiscuous Yalda.

Mother and son enter washroom washes their face, Farida says to Fazal, my body is so wet with your sperm and saliva all over my body, Fazal bent to kiss his mother cunt, and says, mom you asked for vehement sex and beer, and I gave you both, Farida intoxicated she kisses her son, and say, as always you give me the best fuck, Farida takes a quick cold water bath thoroughly washes her vagina, she then dresses up, Fazal wears clothes, and steps out of his mother bedroom.

Fazal approaches Yalda in her room, Fazal holds Yalda's hand and says, my mother has given her consent and thereby pave the way for us to get married, Yalda reacts, by saying, oh honey you made me so happy, ever since the day I step in your house as bride of your father, I had crush on you, I always wanted to be your life partner, Fazal laughs, says, sweeties I too had intense love affection for you, Yalda overjoyed, she changes her mood, darling this is the most precious moment of my life, let us celebrate,

Fazal ask, How? Yalda opens up, she removes her clothes, says, here my darling husband Fazal, see this is me standing full nude in front of you, Fazal says, oh sweeties, I have seen you nude so many times, Yalda replies, today is special and today at this moment let me give you special sex, Fazal, raises his eyebrows, says, wow, darling what is so special about today's sex? Yalda kisses Fazal and says, undress remove your clothes and sleep on bed, Fazal does what Yalda has told him to do, Yalda say till this day we've not done one sex activity which I will perform for you today, Fazal smiles sexy do it quickly, Yalda says "blow-job" I will take your peni in my mouth, Yalda gives oral sex to Fazal, while doing oral sex, Fazal lost in memory world he thinks of his mother who has just few moment ago given him oral sex, Fazal is thrilled happy beyond limit, Fazal give Yalda a fuck copulate.

Fazal ask Yalda, are you happy to hear this news? Are you happy, now that you'll become my wife and we will legitimately enjoy our life together as husband and wife.

Oh what happened? Yalda just had fantastic sex, now, Yalda gets emotional, she explains to Fazal, it's always a privilege for a woman to get married to someone she loves, Yalda adds, I feel overwhelmingly privileged that you are proposing me to marry you, but don't you know that I'm a widow, apart, I'm twice married already, my first marriage was a chaotic affair as my first husband was greedy and loutish person and finally my married to him ended in a bitter divorce, my second marriage to your father "Adil" was a bliss affair, but my happiness was short lived as my husband and your father died an untimely death, Yalda further tells Fazal, now you want me to marry you, I'm profoundly scare, my conscience decision is that I must say no to your proposal.

Fazal queries, do you love me? Yalda nods her head in agreement.

Fazal preaches her, ,……. "The past should be past & stay there, It destroys the Future, Live Life for what tomorrow has to offer not for what has happen yesterday."

Yalda gives a sweet smile and looks into Fazal's eyes, Fazal ask, what do you smell in my body and from my mouth, Yalda replies, from your body I smell courage and power, and from your mouth, I smell, she stops, Fazal ask tell me what smell you getting right now from my mouth? Yalda laughs, softly says, alcohol, Fazal hugs Yalda, than goes inside kitchen and comes back with couple of bottles of beer, Fazal opens one for himself, Fazal queries, my wife would like to enjoy beer, Yalda baffle she hesitate, than say No, Fazal says okay, Yalda quickly says actually I won't mind a beer, Fazal laughs, Yalda says I am so used to smell of beer and wine, your daddy used to drink beer and wine, sometime in romantic mood your daddy used to give me glass of wine to drink, when I give you lip kiss the smell of beer from your mouth is fascinating, Fazal says, lot of mischief in your eyes, you sly woman, but I love you, Yalda says, in your house I have got so much love, money and sex, I count myself fortunate to be married in your family.

Fazal brags, my father was gem of a person, he was great, my father (Adil) taught us to live life with fun and positive energy, Yalda sheepishly looks down and whispers, you mother is also very modern she as well enjoys wine and beer, and she is very beautiful, Fazal in high spirit comments, my mother is hot sexy, she loves to live life with fun, Yalda says, will you go on praising your parents, or will you think of my fun and pleasure as well, Fazal we just had sex what more fun you want, Yalda points her finger towards the table on which beer bottle is kept, darling give me alcohol, give me beer I want to get high on spirits, Fazal nods his head, yes, I will that bottle is for you, but first disrobe yourself, take off the shirt you wearing and remove the panty from your body, Yalda says, oh honey you give drink with condition, I am always happy to be nude for you, Yalda opens up disrobe herself, stands nude, Fazal in sexy mood, opens bottle of beer, pours quarter of the beer on Yalda body, tells her I am wetting you with beer, than hands her the bottle of beer, Yalda finishes beer ask for one more bottle of beer, Fazal with pleasure serve his wife to be Yalda beer,, Yalda request my honey Fazal give me a fuck, here I am on bed with my legs wide spread, put your dick in my pussy, Fazal and Yalda spend quality time romancing.

After romance and sex is over, Yalda covers her head with chador, and conveys her feelings to her man, she says to Fazal, I'm yours and want to always remain yours forever, I accept your proposal to become your wife and to become your better half. Fazal thanks Yalda, and starts his marriage preparation.

Fazal marriage to Yalda is a low key affair, in the presences of few close family friends and relatives, the local Kazi (Muslim Priest) performs Nikah (wedding ritual) ceremony, Yalda becomes bride for the third time and Fazal khan Bangash becomes groom for the first time, Their Wedding is solemnize, Fazal's mother and his siblings are ecstatic and happily accepts Yalda from their stepmother's role to now in the new role of sister-in-law.

Yalda and Fazal makes a new beginning of their life, both Yalda and Fazal are happy to be living as husband and wife, Yalda always ensures that Fazal remains in good humour, she cooks delicious food for her husband.

One Friday morning after overnight bodily pleasure, Yalda gives a body jolt to her husband "Fazal" reminds him its late morning and we are late today in waking up, Fazal romantically says, Did the sun just came out or did you just smile at me, Yalda wears her gown kisses Fazal and says, stop flattering come wake up get fresh and come down in the living room.

Yalda walks downstairs, she listen someone rung a door bell, she request her sister-in-law "Firdoz" to open the main entrance door, Firdoz obliges, she walks to the entrance door with her younger step sister Heena in tow, Firdoz opens the door, she sees a tall man standing at the doorstep, he wishes a loud As-Salamu-Alaykhum, Yalda from distance listens to the voice of the guest and she recognizes the surprise guest by his voice, Yalda rushes to the main entrance door of her house yelling "Walay-Kum-As-Salam," the surprise guest is Yalda's dearest cousin brother "Sadaf Ahmad."

Yalda warmly greets her cousin brother and escorts him inside her house, Yalda is excited to meet her cousin brother, Yalda and Sadaf happily converse and exchanges pleasantries, few moments later Yalda's husband Fazal emerges, she introduces her husband "Fazal to her cousin "Sadaf", Yalda tells Fazal, this man Sadaf Ahmad is my mother's sister's son, and he is as good as my own brother, I have tremendous affection for "Sadaf," Yalda boast about her cousin brother to her husband, she says, Sadaf is a very well verse, well read and learned man, he has travelled to many parts of the world, Fazal comprehends his wife's views.

Fazal strikes instant chord with his wife's cousin brother, they both are intellectual bloke, hence Fazal and Sadaf have lot to talk about and they discusses and converse wide range of topics.

After having good strong breakfast together, Fazal sights an opportunity in his brother-in-law, Fazal is long craving to give his life a whole new dimension, he wants to achieve his objectives in life as he wants to do something radically different in life, Fazal in his mind things that Sadaf Ahmad would be an appropriate man to give him the right guidance.

Fazal request Sadaf to come with him on a long drive and to see the Afghan countryside, Sadaf can't say no to Fazal who is apparently his brother-in-law.

Chapter 7

Fazal takes his wife's cousin brother "Sadaf" far away from Kabul city on the top of the mountain, in pristine environment at high altitude landscape where the sun is falling on the brink of the hill.

Fazal purpose of bring his brother-in-law to such high altitude locale is to have a high altitude discussion.

Fazal tells to Sadaf, my purpose of bring you here at this exotic locale right on the top of this isolated hilly mountain is to discuss some sensitive topics, Sadaf in response make loud hum sound, Sadaf assures, I'll render my unflinching support to you, after all you are my dear cousin sister's dear husband, Fazal laughs and hugs Sadaf, says, thanks, my brother-in-law.

Fazal begins talking his mind, he says to Sadaf, my life is in excruciating limbo, things are basically not happening as I want to in my life, Fazal adds, I am eccentric and extraordinary man, hence my objectives which I want to achieve are also extraordinary.

Sadaf listens to Fazal, than ask him, please be more perspicuous, what exactly you want, how can I help you? Fazal replies, look for the past few years, I've been running my family business, I'm in a business of trading in cement and paints in Kabul, but this is not what I want to do in life, I have set some higher goal and higher targets for myself.

Sadaf enquires, as in, what do you mean? Fazal responses, I want to do something radically different, I am young man, my age is just Twenty years, and I have long future ahead of me, I want to stay ahead of curve and not fall behind the curve.

Sadaf replies, it reflects a very oppressed and depressed state of your mind and soul, Fazal agrees, I think you've guessed it correct.

Sadaf suggest, from what I can understand, you'll be able to achieve your objective either by becoming a politician or you'll have to enter perilous intimate world, Sadaf ask, are you willing to play with fire? Fazal nods his head, yes, you've now hit the nail, this is precisely what I want to do, I am ready to play with fire.

Sadaf queries, but, why? If I may know from you, why do you want to take undue risk? Why are you desperate to play with fire? Don't you know you've recently got married and also you have great responsibility on your shoulder of taking care of your family, which is considerably big.

Fazal replies, my dear brother-in-law, I need help and you seems to be the right person who can assist me, I'm not averse to taking odd **incremental risk**, Fazal adds, look, let me be perspicuous, what I want in life is power and money, I want to explore the world, I want to travel around to discover the world, I want greater exposure to life, hence I want to meet people connect with them learn about their mind set.

Fazal explains to Sadaf, there is immanent risk at every step of our life, hence fearing risk to my life, I don't want the fear of death to be impediment to me in achieving my objectives.

Sadaf after listening to his brother-in-law's brave ambitious views, responses, by clapping, Sadaf claps his hands and compliments Fazal for his brave and determine endeavour.

Sadaf explains his side of the story to Fazal, he say to Fazal, let me briefly tell you few things about myself, Fazal nods his head, says, excellent, let me hear few things about you, about you from you.

Sadaf says, I entered this perilous world of terrorism because of acute poverty, I was unemployed and desperate for money, a local Islamic cleric advised me, that, if I entered the intimate world of terrorism, I'll get lucrative opportunity to make lots of money and thereby my family's and my poverty will eradicate permanently.

Sadaf adds, that religious cleric used his influence and got me inducted in a small terrorist group, Sadaf says, I began my career as a Mujahidin (jihadist struggler) and being a combative Mujahideen for few years, Sadaf says, I later in my life along with an associate branched out on my own, Nowadays, I have become an arms dealer or to says arms and ammunition broker, I and few of my friends supply combative weapons to many terrorist organization in Afghanistan and Pakistan.

Fazal responses, ok, so, Sadaf, I heard your side of the story and I've found it interesting, now that I've heard you and you've heard me and I have made it clear to you my intentions, now you tell me, how will you help me achieve my objectives?

Sadaf replies, yes, my cousin sister's husband, I can see it in your eyes you've incredible talent and you're determine in achieving your objectives, hence I'll no longer try to dissuade you for entering the ever so dangerous intimate world of crimes and terror.

Fazal responses, thank you "brother," Sadaf ask Fazal, you tell me, what role you would like to play? Do you have something in your mind with regards to what you would like to do, you too may have got some idea at least, if you tell me exactly, what's cooking in your mind? Then, accordingly I find the way out for you. Sadaf sarcastically ask, as you desire to enter perilous world of crimes, a profession which will keep you long distance away from your home, you will have to travel and potentially live in hiding, Sadaf adds, you are young man young blood just married, you have young beautiful women in your house young wife and also young mother, young women need young men, Fazal stares at Sadaf, he simply smiles, and says, am not worried, the women of my house are sexually satisfied.

Fazal comprehends Sadaf's view, he says, yes, I'll tell you, Fazal comments, see, I don't want to become a combative Mujahidin (jihadist fighter), Fazal says, I want to learn the administration skills of the Terror world, I want to become a sort of **wheeler dealer**, where in I get opportunity to meet many different kinds and types of people, I want to do work that's challenging and exciting.

Sadaf comprehends Fazal, Sadaf replies, ok, I've understood, and I have thought of an idea for you, so that you get excellent lucrative opportunity to earn money as well as get opportunity to connect with people.

Fazal says, yes, please, disclose you thoughts with regards to me, Sadaf replies, you'll have to enrol yourself in terrorist training camp, this training camp is equivalent to university course, Fazal laughs, ok, so, even the terrorist have to do a masters degree course, hah, hah, hah, Sadaf vociferate, yes, what you thought? That terrorism is a child's play, all the terrorist have to go through intense training before they are given responsibility of carrying out combative attack on either civilian or government security targets, Sadaf add, people are this days seeing terrorism as good professional opportunity, as there's a good opportunity to make good amount of money and also enjoy perks and benefits hence many qualified youngster by their own choice seek entrance in this terror world.

Fazal acknowledges the fact, he says, now, as I have made up my mind to take plunge in this perilous terror world, what is it that I'll have to do?

Sadaf ask Fazal, are you willing to travel all the way to Somalia? Fazal shockingly ask, why? That location is too far away, isn't there any place close by, isn't there some place close to Afghanistan, where I can get training?

Sadaf nods his head in disagreement, Sadaf explains to Fazal, as you are intending to learn skills about Terrorist Administration as in you want to learn how the terrorist organization should be manage and how to deal and to negotiate terrorist attacks, Fazal response with loud, yes, exactly, this is what I want to learn.

Sadaf replies, for you to learn the terror administrative skills, you'll have to travel all the way to Somalia, Fazal again ask, why? Sadaf explains, I'm insisting you to travel all the way to Somalia is because there is a large terror training camp, wherein that terror training camp large number of the "Fedayeen and Mujahideen" (jihadist fighters and the people who voluntarily wants to sacrifice their life for religious purpose) are given intense and rigorous training to fight all sorts of combative forces.

Sadaf further adds, but, that's, not all, the purpose of me recommending you the Somalia terror training camp is because the top instructor or to say the master who gives training to the potential jihadist fighters and his name is "Waqar Iqbal," this gentleman Waqar is a very good friend of mine, I have excellent rapport with him, that's why he "Waqar" would be an ideal trainer for you, plus he will also provide you good earning opportunity as well.

Fazal khan Bangash agrees, ok, as you wish, Fazal queries, how long will I have to stay away from my family and in Somalia? Sadaf replies, at least 6 months, my friend Waqar will train you to perfection, Sadaf add, I'll write a letter to my friend "Waqar" explaining to him everything in detail about you, so that accordingly he'll train you about terrorist activities.

Fazal emphatic reply, done deal, Fazal add, as you may know about my family and myself, we are a very secular and liberal family, we like listening to music wear western clothes respect every religion, I mean to say we are socially progressive family, that's how my late father "**Mr Adil Bangash**" has brought us up.

Fazal further tells to Sadaf, look you happen to be my wife Yalda's cousin brother close blood relative, I want to say it straight to you, that, my family and I are thorough secular, we intensely disregard Islam and dislike Muslims, we are liberal honest educated people, we believe in democracy, my mother, my sisters, and my wife wear fashionable clothes, my sisters wear short length dresses, my mother and wife enjoy drinking beer, Sadaf carefully listens to Fazal, then, Sadaf puts his hand on Fazal's shoulder and says, everything you just told me, let me inform you I already knew it, my sister Yalda had briefed me given detail information about you and your family lifestyle. Sadaf moves very close to Fazal, and softly says, Islam is mother fucking mega scam, even I hate Islam, I am what I am a Mujahidin only for the purpose to make money, else I hate fucking Qurans and hadiths, Muslims are stone worshipers.

Sadaf smirks, response, I understand you and your families social status, I'm aware that your family practices moderate and liberal value, Fazal makes loud hum sound, Sadaf explains, "***we human don't have to be internally the same as we are externally***," Sadaf teaches Fazal, learn to adopt yourself as the circumstances warrants, we have to learn the art of adopting various different moods and learn to follow different protocol as the situation demands.

Fazal acknowledges, yes, my dear brother-in-law, I have imbibe everything you said and have briefed me about, that's enough information for me to know, now let us get the ball rolling, tell me, when do I plan my trip to notoriously dangerous locale in the world, the perilous "Somalia"?

Sadaf Ahmad says, yes, indeed, Sadaf explains to Fazal, I'll communicate to my good friend "Waqar Iqbal" about you and your aspiration, also let me tell you a bit about who this gentleman "Waqar," he "Waqar" is an Saudi national, he is in his mid-forties, and even though he (Waqar) preaches hard core fundamentalist religious belief and entice and encourages others to take up arms and fight the infidel army, but quite ironically he (Waqar) is personally a gem of a person, he is extremely progressive and broad minded and like you (referring to Fazal) he too is a liberal.

Fazal comments, wow, that's nice that, I'll have privilege of working under the apprenticeship of a considerate person like "Waqar Iqbal," Sadaf response, yes, my friend Waqar will teach you every nitty-gritty of terror world, and you'll enjoy staying in the terror training camp, in the training camp there's lot of extra curricula fun.

Sadaf says, ok, now let me tell you, most important thing which you as well are curious to know, Fazal nods his head, yes, please tell me, when I have to join the terror camp in Somalia? Sadaf comments, five days from today a batch of six Mujahideen will leave for Somalia from Pakistani city of "Peshawar", this batch of six so-called Mujahideen are fresh recruits and are being inducted in jihadist group as combative armed militias.

Sadaf tells Fazal, you'll have to travel to Peshawar in Pakistan in next four days and join this group, than along with six of the fresh recruit you will leave for Somalia, your journey will be long and treacherous, as y'all will have to travel all the way to Somalia in all mode of transport like road than railway than sea than again by road to reach your final destination in the bushy thick forest area of Somalia where the terror camp is actually located.

Fazal reacts, with sheepish smirk and looks up in sky than says, oh goodness my journey to intimate world, will be adventurous.

Sadaf comments, yes, this is what the bad intimate world is all about, one has to travel and learn to live all the way in treacherous rugged terrain.

Fazal says, doesn't matter to me, I'm ready to walk that difficult path to achieve my objectives, Sadaf comments, "**fortune favours the bold**," Fazal replies, I agree with these words of yours, that you just said "100%."

Sadaf Ahmad hugs and wishes his brother-in-law great success in his endeavour, Fazal and his wife's cousin brother "Sadaf" concludes there long meeting on optimistic note and heads back down the hill slope to Kabul city, back to Fazal's home.

Fazal and Sadaf have returned home its late afternoon, Yalda lay's down plates on the dining table and serves exquisite cuisine that she has prepared for her dotting husband and her dearest cousin brother "Sadaf," Fazal and Sadaf enjoys there lunch together.

After having lunch Sadaf hands an envelope to Fazal and tells him, inside the envelope is the contact details of a Man whose name is "Mir Wasim Rahimi" whom you have to contact in Pakistani city of Peshawar, Sadaf add, "Wasim Rahimi" is the man who has been given the responsibility by Known Sunni Jihadi organization "**The' Al Noora**," to escort the fresh batch of Mujahideen (jihadi fighters) to Somalia terror training camp, Sadaf says to Fazal, you have to meet this gentleman "Mir Wasim Rahimi" in Peshawar and later he'll take care of you and will take you along with him and six other man to Somalia's Jihadi Training Camp, Fazal says, ok, thank you, I'll do exactly the way you've told me.

Sadaf further says, the outside world perceived "Al Noora" as hard core fundamentalist Terrorist group, but most people from our community considers "Al Noora" as jihadi organization who are fighting against the infidel forces and infidel ideology, the "Al Noora" is considered to be a jihadist organization promoted to save Islamic religious interest.

Fazal sarcastically laughs and comments, hell bastards, they (Al Noora) save our religion by killing the infidels, who are they to decide who's infidel? What rights do stone and idols worshipers Muslims have to take innocent lives.

Sadaf puts his hands on Fazal's shoulder and nods his head in disagreement, Sadaf makes Fazal understands by saying, "**When in Rome do what the Romans do**" Sadaf adds, please hold your thoughts keep your secular perception and conviction to yourself, be careful, ensure no one gets a whiff about your liberal and secular thoughts, Sadaf explains to Fazal, you are by your own choice taking a plunge in a dangerous world of Terrorism, one mistake and these bastards Islamists people will not give you a second chance to regret.

Fazal commits, yes, my brother-in-law, I'm a matured man, I will ensure not to let anyone know about my internal thoughts and feelings.

Sadaf says, that will be good, Sadaf says, also before I go let me tell you that the person who will groom you in terror training camp "Waqar Iqbal" is one among four supreme commander of "Al Noora jihadist group," Sadaf add, I'll speak to Waqar over phone as well as correspond with him and explain to him in detail everything regarding you, Fazal replies, Thank you.

Early evening Sadaf after spending few moments drinking tipple beer with his cousin sister Yalda, and playing with her daughter "Heena," Sadaf departs from the house of Fazal and goes to his hometown **Gadrez.**

Chapter 8

With mounting concern one morning, after breakfast, Fazal request his mother and his wife "Yalda" to spare few moments with him, as he has to disclose it to his mother and wife about his all too important mission of traveling to Somalia for rather bizarre purpose.

Fazal's mother "Farida" and his wife "Yalda" leaves there work in kitchen and sits with Fazal to listen to what he has to tell them, Yalda ask, yes, my husband, what's so important thing that you want to discuss with us? Please, tell me, I am curious, Fazal nods his head, with smile on his face he gaze at his mother and wife, than tells them, in life, "desperate time calls for desperate measures," Farida ask, my son, we all are living comfortable life, therefore, where is a desperation? Fazal shrugs off his mother view, he says, no, mamma, for me, life has a lot of meaning, I want to change the dynamics, of my life, I am feeling I am an incomplete human.

Both Yalda and Farida in one voice tells Fazal, please be perspicuous, stop talking in metaphor and proverbs, Fazal responses, ok, mamma and you Yalda, listen to what I have to say, I'm planning an excursion, day after tomorrow, I'll embark on a long journey, and I will be back in Kabul after six months.

Fazal's mother stunned to listen her son's ambitious plan, she ask him, why? Please tell us clearly, what is your plan? Why you have to go on such long journey? Leaving us behind all alone hear in Kabul, there is so much trouble and danger in our country, and you want to leave us women alone in this arguable most dangerous city Kabul and go away for six long months, Fazal replies, mamma and Yalda, please, understand my compulsion, don't ask me more as in where exactly I'm going and for what purpose.

Fazal adds, pray that I succeed in my endeavour and accomplish my dream, whatever I'm doing is for the betterment of our family, we need lots of money so that we can at some stage move away from this perilous country and built our abode in a safe harbour, our family business is sluggish, there is too much competition and demand is low, expenses are rising and cash income dwindling, Fazal's mother stops from talking more and advising her son, but Fazal's wife "Yalda" reacts furiously, she fiercely oppose Fazal's move to go on long excursion, she runs upstairs to her room in disgust, Fazal follows his wife to their bedroom.

Fazal cajoles and tries his best to convince his furious wife, Fazal says, please let me go on a happy note, trust me whatever I'm doing, I'm doing for the betterment of our family, Yalda questions his wisdom, but ,why? You already have a family business, Fazal answers, No, the economy of our country is in excruciating limbo, there's too much uncertainty, everywhere around, and my business fortune is in excruciating slump.

Yalda profusely shed tears and comments, my first marriage was a disaster as my first husband was a monstrous person, my second marriage that to your own father was otherwise a success but it came to an abrupt end when my husband and your father "Adil Bangash" was killed by Muslim terrorists attack.

Yalda continues her tirade, now that I'm married to you and am happy in marriage with you, but now you too are deserting me and going away somewhere far, if something happens to you, what will happen to me? Any answers.

Fazal replies, your point well taken, but there is an immanent risk every step of the way in our life, also as we are big family, and my endeavour is to give each of my family member the best of life, I am determined to give the best comfort to my sisters and mother and wife and children and my brother, and to live life in comfort we need lots of money and to earn money one has to take unprecedented risk in life. It is our bad luck to be born in Islamic country and to live in insular Muslims society, Fazal ask Yalda, do you like Islam and do you feel comfort living with Muslims? Yalda assertive reply, No, Not at all, being submissive wife I like what my husband like and hate what my husband hate, and I know how much you dislike Muslim, Fazal gives a passionate lip kiss to Yalda kisses her bolls and says, yes my wife once I have money we will move out of Islamic country Afghanistan, and go and settle in secular Christian or Hindu nation, where we'll have freedom to eat what we want wear what we like, Yalda says I feel suffocated to live among Muslims.

Fazal has to take immense pain and afford to convince his ever so reluctant wife "Yalda" to allow him to go on long journey, Yalda finally cave-in and so does Fazal's mother, both ladies give there in principle consent to Fazal to embark on his journey and prays for his success.

Fazal only has two nights to spend in Kabul with his family, his devastatingly beautiful wife "Yalda," Fazal ensures to make a most of the time he has left to spend with his wife, Fazal passionately indulges with his wife, gives "Yalda" scintillating sex and chilled beer, Yalda to enjoys bodily pleasure with her husband.

Yalda sheepishly says, darling husband thanks for giving me good time, fantastic SEX, Yalda knows about incest, Yalda reminds Fazal, honey just one night is left, your mother must be eager for fun fantasy, Fazal laughs, Yalda says, go entertain your mother.

The onus is on Fazal to make his mother happy as well, Farida say my darling son, I will miss you so much, you are my son, and love sex as well, Fazal says, just one night is left, let us indulge, Farida say I am in mood to drink wine, the arrangement is made, Fazal and Farida vehemently indulge in sex, high on wine and high on sex,

The day is Tuesday, and today Fazal has to commence his long journey, Fazal spends few hours cosy with his wife "Yalda," he also spends enough time with his sisters and late morning, it's time for Fazal to depart from his house, Fazal hugs his mother and his sisters, he gives a passionate hug to his wife "Yalda" and with his bags all packed, he picks up his luggage and on emotional note but with lots of aspiration Fazal steps out of his house, and starts his excursion into the perilous world of terror.

Fazal reaches Pakistani city of Peshawar, and from the bus station he heads straight to the location where he could find his escort "Mir Wasim Rahimi," Fazal reaches a venue where Wasim stays, Fazal introduces himself to Mir Wasim Rahimi, he gives Wasim reference of his close relative "Sadaf Ahmad," Wasim Rahimi acknowledges and graciously greets Fazal and tells him, that Sadaf has called and spoken to him with regards to you, Wasim tells Fazal, we've to leave for Somalia early Thursday morning, he makes arrangement for Fazal accommodation and request him to feel comfortable and take sufficient rest, so as to be fit enough to undertake at least four to five day long journey that will commence day after tomorrow.

Fazal thanks Wasim Rahimi, Wasim informs Fazal, that his cousin brother-in-law "Sadaf Ahmad" is a very dear friend of mine, hence it's my responsibility to give a special attention to you, Fazal replies, oh, that's, very kind of you.

Chapter 9

The dawn breaks out, the day is Thursday, Fazal khan Bangash is ready with his bags and luggage, Mir Wasim Rahimi approaches Fazal in his room and request him to board a big private vehicle as its time for us to commence journey, Wasim Rahimi preaches Fazal and Six other young men that we are starting our journey in the name of "Almighty God," and our ultimate purpose is to defeat the infidel forces the enemies of our religion, save for Fazal the remaining men yell in one voice "InshaAllah" Ameen," one of the boy a potential (Mujahideen) in great euphoria shout it's our privilege and almighty has bestowed great honour on us few to die fighting against the infidel, Mir Wasim Rahimi comprehends the youth's spirit to sacrifice his life to save our religion.

The driver starts the vehicle, and a long journey from Peshawar to the jungles of Somalia.

While Fazal is sitting in the vehicle feeling lonely encumbered with all sorts of thoughts, back home in Kabul his beloved wife “Yalda” feels giddy, her mother-in-law “Farida” takes her to the lady doctor’s clinic, the doctor performs few medical test on Yalda, after seeing the test report, the doctor informs Yalda and Farida that the stork has visited.

Yalda is declared pregnant, she’s carrying child of Fazal Khan Bangash, Fazal’s mother “Farida” reacts with joy and enthusiasm on learning about the news that her daughter-in-law “Yalda” is pregnant and that she would soon become a granny.

Yalda has a mix feelings, she is desperately missing the man whom she loves the most, Yalda can’t share the joy of becoming mother with her husband, Yalda soon reconcile with the harsh reality and carries on with her life.

After nearly six days of travelling, Fazal along with Mir Wasim Rahimi and six other Mujahideen (jihadist fighter) reaches the Rocky Bushy jungle of Somalia, Fazal gets down from the vehicle pulls out his luggage from the vehicle carrier, Wasim tells Fazal to wait out in the open for some time while I make arrangement for your accommodation in this jihadist training camp, Fazal nods his head, ok.

Few moments later Fazal sees a tall healthy man looking like a Hollywood film actor is walking along with Wasim approaching towards him, the handsome man comes close to Fazal greets him with a hug, says, so nice meeting you, welcome to this notorious jihadi training camp, Fazal for a moment spaced out wonders who this gentleman is who is behaving so obsequiously with me, wearing a beaming smile Wasim Rahimi informs Fazal that this handsome man is the boss of this Sunni jihadi training camp his name is “Waqar Iqbal,” Fazal reacts, oh, so, you are, the great “Mr Waqar Iqbal,” Waqar laughs and says, yes, Fazal tells him, my brother-in-law was singing praises of you, hence I was immensely curious about seeing you and meeting you.

Waqar and Fazal exchange pleasantries, Waqar assures Fazal, make yourself comfortable, your brother-in-law "Sadaf" is a dear friend of mine, we both know each other for past many years, Fazal acknowledges, Waqar request Fazal, please have a nice rest and after two days your training will start, Fazal replies, thank you.

Because, Fazal's cousin brother-in-law "Sadaf" has extremely good equation with the man in charge of the jihadist training camp "Waqar Iqbal," hence Fazal enjoys special privileges, a special tent is allotted to Fazal which he shares it with no one else.

Fazal missing his family in Kabul from the Somalian jungle he uses Waqar's satellite telephone to call his home in Afghanistan, Fazal calls his home, his mother answers the call, he ask his mother of her wellbeing than Fazal chats over the phone with his younger sisters "Firdoz, Zarine and "Heena" with whom he has unique dual relationship of stepbrother as well as stepfather, later a big moment, the phone receiver is handed to his wife "Yalda," Yalda passionately converse with her husband "Fazal" both inquires about each other's health, Yalda tells, I miss you a lot, Fazal replies, same feeling here, even I miss you, now, Yalda is above to break a big news.

Yalda says, guess, what? Fazal ask, what? My submissive wife, Yalda replies, in this moment of glory you are far away from me, Fazal sensible enough, understands what his wife means by saying "moment of glory," Fazal romantically ask, please, my loving wife, let me hear from yourself itself, what is that moment of glory? Yalda sheepishly comments, you naughty boy, as if you don't know, Fazal swoon, tell me, I am getting curious, Yalda says, than listen, we are soon going to become proud parents, stork has visited me.

Fazal excited to listen, his wife's comments, Fazal thrill to hear that soon he would become a "Daddy," Yalda breaks down and starts crying, she tells Fazal, I miss you so much, can't you understand a woman's feeling, Specially at a time when she's conceive and above to become mother, Fazal consoles his wife, he says, this are very challenging time and we need to be forbearance and hold our nerves, Yalda and understand how much Fazal loves her and he's doing whatever he is doing for the betterment of their family, Fazal assures Yalda, soon, everything will be fine and we'll all together live happy life, on happy note, Fazal concludes his telephonic conversation.

After having long distance phone conversation and informing Fazal that all their heavy sex activities have borne results, and now she is pregnant, and Fazal will soon become father, Yalda walks to living room, she sees her mother-in-law and sister-in-law Firdoz are having conversation, Firdoz see Yalda entering the room, she gets up with big smile on her face, Firdoz greets Yalda hold her hand and makes her sit next to her on sofa, Farida tells so my beautiful sexy daughter-in-law, you must be happy feeling good talking to your husband and informing him about your pregnancy, both Firdoz and Yalda grins, Yalda say, yes, I am happy. Firdoz with joy comments, I am so lucky my father and brothers are liberal, secular, my daddy gave us freedom to live life the way we want, Firdoz says, mom, we are fortunate, but outside on streets I see Muslims living in fear, women are suppressed, women cannot eat the food they like, Muslim females are not allowed to wear clothes they want to, Firdoz thanks her parents for being liberal secular.

Firdoz makes bold statement, mummy, let me tell you, I will Not marry a Muslim, Muslim men objectify their wives, suppresses their wife and daughters, I will marry a non-Muslim or I will remain unmarried, Farida thoughts wandering, she is stunned listening her daughter bold decision, but, Yalda sitting next to Firdoz is ecstatic, Yalda says, fantastic you are bold and beautiful, Yalda says yes mummy (Farida is now Yalda's mother-in-law, so Yalda now calls her mummy) she (Firdoz) is taking a right stand, Farida smiles you young girls are bold, Farida ask Yalda, why you so emphatically supporting Firdoz decision of not marrying a Muslim man? Yalda stands up she strolls around and then sits next to Farida, Yalda tells, Muslim men either become terrorist and die or they die in terror attacks, and we women are left alone with no one to care for us, Firdoz nods her head and comprehend Yalda's view, yes, Muslim men insular and Muslim men life is always uncertain, Yalda justify and proves it, if we walk around Afghan and Pakistan cities there we find hundreds of thousands of women who are widowed or their husbands have left them and run away, so many Muslim women single mother.

Farida gets emotional she tells her daughter Firdoz to come close to her, Firdoz sits close to her mother, Farida hugs and kisses Firdoz, Farida says, yes, true these men disregards their wives and daughters, I am fortunate to have married to a man (Adil) who as honest sensible kind hearted person, but he died, Muslim terrorist killed him, and now I am left alone, I am young in my forties and become widow, Firdoz wipes tears falling from her mother's eyes, Yalda also become emotional, but, Yalda maintains silence, Farida tells her daughter Firdoz, I give my consent to both you sisters you and Zarine, marry who you like, I give my full support to both my daughters.

Firdoz kisses her mother, and says, thank you mamma, Yalda claps, wow, that's an good chemistry between you mother and daughters, Yalda further adds, I always keep saying, I am so happy to be married in your family, you folks are fantastic people.

Farida says, our society was not always like what it is today, in old generations, my mother and grandmothers used to enjoy freedom, once Afghanistan was a free country people had human rights, my mother had so many friends from Hindu community, in old times men and women could freely enjoys smoking Hookah, cigar, and drink wine and beer, my grandmothers used to wear Midi Dress, Farida adds, my paternal grandmother used to smoke cigar and drink wine, we were liberal secular society. Firdoz ask, mamma than, what happen? Why we become so regressive and backwards society? Farida says it is all politics, the Islamic Mullahs, and Islamists politicians and the Wahhabis have destroyed secular fabric and made our society backwards, in name of religion making women wear full black clothes, stoning women to death, killing innocent people. This is precisely reason why your daddy, brothers and I hate Islam and dislike Muslims, Firdoz angry, yes the Muslim terrorists killed my daddy, I hate Islam, Yalda echoes, yes, Islamic Jihadis killing innocent humans, stoning women to death, even I dislike Muslims.

Thousands miles away from Kabul, Fazal spends a whole day in confinement of his tent that has been allotted to him, Fazal in the evening strolls around in the jihadist training camp, the camp is huge, spread in Hundreds of acres, Fazal walks alone around the jihadist training camp, and he witnesses hundreds of youth in different batches taking all kinds of training in arms combative and explosive as well as suicide bomb explosion training, Fazal also witness many jihadi fighters enjoying themselves having extra curricula fun.

Fazal finds an isolated spot in camp and sits on a small rock, Fazal sits on the rock and thinks hard, he tells to himself, what a place damn bad I have landed myself in. He thinks, but, I'm not bemoaning, this excursion of mine in this remote Somalian jungle is like an adventurous Camping or a picnic, I will enjoy my stay here in this bizarre location with intimate peoples around.

Third day of Fazal's stay in Sunni jihadi camp, Waqar calls Fazal early morning in his room and request Fazal to meet him in person after breakfast, Waqar tells Fazal, from today onwards I'll start grooming you, Fazal replies, Thank you, I am ready to go, Waqar replies, ok, great, so meet me later, and let's get things started, Fazal confirms, ok, sir.

Late morning after breakfast, Waqar after doing his regular physical workout exercise, he calls Fazal close to him, standing in the open field, Waqar queries with Fazal, so, how did you like our jihadi training camp? Fazal laughs, this is an adventure of my life, though I have no precise answer to your question, whether I liked this jihadist camp or not, Fazal says, I'm here by my own choice, it's not important for me to comment whether I like this jihadist training camp or not, my purpose of coming in this Somalian jungle is not to entertain myself, I have objectives to achieve in my life, and that's precisely the reason why I'm here standing in front of you.

Waqar compliments, excellent reply, I can judge it from your body language, you are no ordinary man, you are man of substance, Fazal replies, *passive aggression sends wrong message*, I'm a pragmatic assertive person.

Waqar puts both his hands on Fazal's shoulder and says, come let us go further away from this training camp, let us sit in isolation, I've a lot to discuss with you, Fazal says, ok, let us move, Fazal and Waqar Iqbal walks a distance, they reach a place where there is a small river flowing, in the shadow of the tree on the side of the river they sit to hold high volte meeting.

Waqar tells, wow, ideal location, don't you think so, Fazal sitting on the rock in this river water, surrounded by rocky mountain and thick bushy trees, in the bright sunshine, for the two of us to make sensitive conversation discuss intimate topics, Fazal smirks, make hum sound.

Waqar starts conversation, says, your close relatives and my good friend "Sadaf" has explained to me everything about you and your objectives and your motives in life.

Waqar ask, I want to now listen from your mouth, as in, why have you decided to select perilous profession? Don't you know the outside world perceived us jihadis as "Terrorist," and they bar us from travelling inside their country and there is an immanent risk every step of our way.

Fazal replies, yes, obviously I'm well and truly aware of immanent peril, Fazal add, I want to gain power and wealth, that are my objectives.

Waqar response, interesting, what else? Fazal add, simply surviving to live life is No fun to me, I want to thrive through my encounters with other people, and enrich myself and my family.

Waqar queries, what do you understand by Islamic Sunni jihad movement? Fazal smiles, and replies, the meaning of "Jihad," it means a clever ploy by shrewd and intelligent person or persons "like you me" and few others cunning persons to hoodwink the large whimsical population of the world, basically we've to, bluff our way out to achieve our objectives.

Waqar overwhelmingly impressed by Fazal's opinions, Waqar reacts, you're amazing young man, you don't need any particular training, Waqar adds, you are audacious man.

Fazal inquires, what do you mean? By saying, I don't need any kind of training, Waqar response, you have proved to me your mettle, you are **proficient and perspicacious person**, Fazal says, thank you for the compliments.

Waqar tells Fazal, as you are interested in learning the administrative part of terrorism tactics, basically you want to play a "liaise" (a go in between), Fazal nods his head, yes, Waqar explains, in terrorism administrative, one needs to have excellent elocutionary skills, besides that, what's most important is that a person needs to be intellectually brilliant, as you said earlier, we need to bluff our way out.

Waqar says, I'll give you some opportunity to strike deals, Fazal ask, as in, Waqar replies, as in, as you can see we run huge jihadi terrorists and criminal or to say mafia network, and plus, we also carry out combative strikes, we carry out terror attacks, Waqar adds, we are as well running our "Al Noora" jihadi organization, and to run organization we as well need money and lots of money, we have to pay our jihadi fighters monthly salary plus when our jihadi fighters gets killed in combative operation or during suicide attacks, we have to pay heavy compensation to their family.

Fazal comprehends, than ask, ok, I listened to you and have understood your jihadi movement business activities, Fazal ask, now let me know, how is your organization's "Al Noora" funded? Means, how do y'all raise money? What is your source of finances? Waqar replies, good question, see, we raise funds from multiple sources and from multiple activities.

Waqar further elaborates, our jihadi organization receives money as donations from governments that sympathize with us, obviously these governments belongs to our religion Sunni Islam, but there donation isn't sufficient enough, Waqar add, on the flip side, we also have to pay bribes to many governments to win their favour, so, we raise most of our financial resources from underworld activities or to say "grey trade" we are involved in trading in Narcotics plus we also have business interest in sports that is "**Match Fixing**," Fazal frowns, oh, really, what sports do y'all "Fix," Waqar answers, yes, we mainly Fix "Football Matches" and also at times we Fix "Boxing Games" as well, and also we take assignment to explode explosive, there are many vested interest who sabotage against their own people their own community, hence they hire us for the service to carry out snuck attack and also contract killings.

Fazal response, oh, that's fantastic, Waqar reacts, isn't it challenging and interesting profession, Fazal nods, oh, yes, fascinating and challenging profession, Waqar agrees, yes, indeed ours is a very thrilling and action packed profession that's the reason so many qualified youths, "Boys/girls" are these days by their own choice enrolling themselves in the world of Terror.

Waqar queries, what is your favourite sports? Fazal laughs, my favourite sports is Cricket, Waqar thrilled, oh really, your favourite sport is Cricket, Waqar comments, what a co-incident, my favourite sport is cricket as well, Fazal replies, how so exciting we both are cricket buff.

Waqar says to Fazal, what I will do is give you an opportunity to meet our clients and sly contacts and give you complete free hand in striking the deals on behalf of my Al Noora jihadist organization, this will give you direct exposure to our nefarious trade practice and you'll also learn many secrets of our intimate profession.

Fazal replies, how nice of you "brother," Waqar says to Fazal, trust me you'll enjoy working for my outfit "Al Noora jihadi organization."

Fazal replies, fascinating stuff, but tell me, why is there so much hatred among people of this world? It really pains me to see so much of human blood getting wasted.

Waqar replies, please no emotion, in our intimate profession, Fazal response, well, to let you know, as a person, what I am externally, am not the same internally, Fazal explains, I am secular and liberal, my family my parents are secular, liberal, my wife and sisters are feminists.

Waqar comments, please don't let your internal "you" come out of you, you have to be reticent about your motives, Fazal agrees, yes, I am aware of it.

Waqar says, have a listen, cunning people like us for past thousands of years have ensured that a large section of the society remains "intellectually duffer," our endeavour is to ensure that these section of society never get intellectually entrenched, because once these section of society gain knowledge and starts to understand the real politics that's played beyond the scene our game will get over,

Waqar gets up, walks around looks in every direction to ensure No one is around, Waqar then sits, very close to Fazal, and whispers in his ears, listen my young brother, Islam is a fucking mega political scam, and spiritual gimmick, all the Islamic characters so-called prophet Muhammad and the Qurans are all fiction fairy tale stories..

Fazal gaze into Waqar's eyes, says, very interesting conversation we're having, please tell me more, Waqar elaborates, to ensure that a large section of society in this world on this planet remains "Dum duffers" and to ensure that cunning and shrewd people like us keep prospering, Fazal ask, yes, what?

Waqar says, the various religions and religious beliefs are nothing but "Sham," Fazal agrees, oh, yes, I'm in full agreement with you, this aspect that, the religion are nothing but "Sham" I'd realize when I was 8 years old.

Waqar response, exactly, this is what I mean, when we remind people about their religion and once we are able to convince people that what religion they belong to and what are the belief and principles of their religion, these same mad deranged people when time comes, they never ever hesitate even one bit, to lay down their life, and never ever hesitate even for a moment to take someone else's life, Fazal agrees, very true.

Waqar explains, religion and racism are such tools, that it gives us selfish cunning people to emotionally blackmail the naïve section of our society and propel them into wrongdoings.

Fazal tells, fascinating, I thoroughly enjoyed the time I have spent with you, Waqar assures Fazal, you are my responsibility and it's going to be my job to ensure that you thrive professionally, Fazal thanks Waqar, there meeting concludes.

Fazal ask Waqar, will it be fine with you if I personally interact with this so-called Mujahideen (jihadi fighters) in the training camp? Fazal adds, I want to interact with few of these stupid guys to understand there mind set, Waqar replies, of course, but, you've to ensure that your liberal and secular thoughts doesn't emanates, else it could spell trouble, Fazal assures, I'll mince my words before I speak, Waqar gives his nod, Ok.

Chapter 10

Fazal a reclusive and a very private person, spends most of his time alone in isolation, Fazal has made few friends specially from Kenya and Pakistani national in the jihadist training camp with whom he plays his favourite sports Cricket.

One day late morning, Fazal decides to interact with few trainee Mujahideens (jihadist fighters), to understand from them as to why are they willing to sacrifice their life if at all need be. Fazal is curious to establish the fact that these boys and few women among them have become Mujahideens by choice or by compulsion.

Fazal approaches a fresh recruit in the jihadist training camp whose names is Nissar who hails from Nigeria, Fazal introduces himself to Nissar and request him to spend few moments with him, Nissar happily obliges and tells Fazal its nice meeting you, Fazal and Nissar finds few empty chairs to sit on, Fazal and Nissar starts with exchanging pleasantries and after brief small talks, Fazal digress the topic, he ask Nissar, so, my friend, what's your age? Nissar replies, I'm only 17 years old, Fazal frowns and ask, ok, at this tender age, you've taken up arms in your hand instead of having books in your hand.

Nissar has a bizarre reason for taking plunge in the intimate world and reason to become terrorist, Nissar explains to Fazal, you want to know the reason, why I've enrol myself in this jihadist training camp and, why? I'm taking dangerous combative arms training, Fazal nods, and says, friend just out of curiosity I've asked you, Nissar replies, never mind friend, listen, from very childhood I'm fascinated towards action, I love watching action packed Hollywood flicks, as I've watched many movies which shows fast car chases and gun battles and sex, seeing so much action in Reel life entice me to make action my profession, hence I took this opportunity of becoming a professional "jihadist fighter."

This profession will not only give me immense job satisfaction but it also provides me an excellent earning opportunity, Fazal listens to what Nissar's talking with eyes wide open, Nissar adds, you know, I'll earn an annual salary of Ten Thousand US dollar, beside this in case of my death, this jihadist organization will handsomely compensate my family, I'll get opportunity to travel plus I'll get free food and accommodation with whichever jihadist organisation or group I work for, this kind of facility "No" corporate job will provide me.

Nissar after completing explaining his reason of becoming professional Jihadist, he ask Fazal, isn't it the right thing I've done by taking plunge into this profession, of becoming a "Mujahideen," Fazal smirks, he's at loss of words, but he comments, excellent plan you have for yourself my friend, please keep it up, Nissar says Thank you, "friend."

Fazal saunters in the jihadist training camp soaking up intensely strong Sun heat, Fazal spots a young man sitting on the branch of a big tree and cleaning his gun, Fazal decides to approach that young man.

Fazal as well climb the tree and first he ensures that the branch of the tree is strong enough to take weight of the strongly built young men, Fazal satisfied the branch is strong enough, he occupies the place next to that young youth, the youth wearing a beaming smile, welcomes Fazal.

Fazal says, young man, what's up? You're sitting alone away from the training camp and polishing your "AK47 Gun," the youth first introduces himself to Fazal as Asif, Fazal in turn introduces himself to Asif, they both exchange pleasantries, Asif informs him, he's from Somalia itself, Fazal says, I'm a Pashtun from Afghanistan, Fazal and Asif starts conversing.

Fazal inquires with Asif, how come, you've landed here in this jihadist training camp? Asif replies, I'm not a trainee any more, I'm a full time jihadist and member of our jihadist group "Al Noora," Fazal acknowledges, ok, he ask Asif, so, if I may ask you "brother"? why have you chosen to become a jihadist? I'm asking you this just out of curiosity, Asif comments, No problem, brother, I'll tell you, why I have by my own choice become a jihadist fighter? The profession which the outside world perceive as "Terrorist," Fazal smiles and makes a hum sound.

Asif elaborates, I became jihadist fighter because I wanted to and want to serve purpose of helping my religion, I want to serve my religion's interest, as you know, these infidels are always trying to suppress the voice of "almighty" the true believers of "Almighty," Asif further add, I hail from a family which passionately follows the religious rule, not only myself many more members from my family and relatives have serve the interest of our esteemed religion.

Asif continues talking and Fazal patiently listens to Asif's comments, Asif add, my father was a jihadist and he happily sacrifice his life fighting against the infidel forces, my brother lost his life serving our religion he was a suicide bomber and on a mission he exploded himself and sacrifice his life.

Asif says, it will be a proud moment for me, the day I lay down my own life fighting for the cause of my great religion, sacrifice my life for my beloved prophet, every infidel I kill it emollient my mind, I'm craving to have this world free of infidels, Fazal reacts sarcastically, oh, yes, it's not only your wish but mine as well, Asif thrill, oh, really, brother, are you, you as well want to get rid of these infidels, and want to have planet with only the believers of our beloved prophet, Fazal rather reluctant replies, yes, brother.

Asif now sheepishly smiles, than says to Fazal, "brother," do you know one very exciting thing? Fazal queries, what? Asif replies, its written in one of our religious holy book, that any man who dies waging jihad against the infidels, the man who becomes a martyr, the doors of heaven opens up, and the jihadist who have killed the infidels in their life time, when the such jihadist die, that particular jihadist is welcomed in heaven by 72 virgins on the doors of heaven, and "he" the jihadist gets entertain in heaven, Asif cravingly ask Fazal, isn't it an excellent deal, that we jihadist when we'll die, we'll be welcomed by 72 virgins.

Fazal doesn't know how to react, Fazal talks to himself in his mind, what an idiot the likes of "Asif's" are, these fools do not understand that they are simply been taken for a ride, Asif jolts Fazal, "brother, where are you lost? Fazal regains his sense than replies, oh, brother, I was lost, I was thinking about those 72 virgins you just talked about, Asif makes fun, oh, that's what you were thinking about, the 72 virgins on the doorsteps of heaven, Asif add, brother, we have to be proud of our self and our prophet that we jihadist will be taken special care of when we die, in the house of almighty.

While Asif is continuing his talk, Fazal see many "Women Mujahideen (jihadist fighters) taking training in the training camp, Fazal once again thinks in his mind, and talks to himself, he thinks" this joker (Asif) sitting next to me, thinks that every jihadist fighter who'll kill the infidel when he dies will be welcome in heaven by 72 virgins, Fazal keeps thinking and talking to himself in his mind, "Now I could see so many women as well in this jihadist camp taking combative training obviously these women will also kill the innocent civilians whom they term as infidels, now when these women jihadist dies will they as well be received and welcome at the doorstep of heaven by 72 virgin men," Fazal thinks should I put this question to this cartoon (Asif) sitting next to me, Fazal decides, No, let me keep my mouth shut, let me stop conversing with this man "Asif" let me go now, Asif ask, "Brother Fazal" where are you lost again, are you again thinking of those 72 virgins on the doorstep of heaven, Fazal to hide his anger and frustration, nods his head, and starts laughing hysterically and Asif as well joins Fazal in laughing with him, Fazal lives Asif sitting on the branch of the tree and he jumps from the branch on to the ground and walks away.

Fazal continues interacting session with few more jihadist in the training camp, Fazal during his interaction session finds out that few of the men or women have become jihadist by their own choice on the pretext of serving the religious cause while few of them have been forced into taking up arms and become jihadist (who are considered terrorist by outside world), some of them have opted to become jihadist because they consider becoming jihadist is a good career option while few of them are influence by action movies and they like action and fights, few of the men whom Fazal spoke to told him, that acute poverty and tense social living condition compel them to plunge in the terror world.

The dusk falls, Fazal feels extremely frustrated from all the stories that he heard thru out the day from different people, diverse people from diverse demographic gave diverse reasons to Fazal, as in, why they have taken up arms in there hand and why they are not averse to killing others and not afraid of dying themselves.

Fazal skips night dinner, instead at night, Fazal sits, outside his tent, and stares at the sky above, the dark sky with stars sparkling, Fazal vividly things, gosh, what a world this is? How naïve most people in this world are? Fazal holds his head with both his hands, Fazal says to himself, let me not "Rack my brain" anymore, my purpose is to achieve my objectives by hook or by crook.

Chapter 11

Few days have passed, for Fazal having arrived at this Somalian jungle in the jihadist training camp of "Al Noora jihadist group," Fazal is waiting for "Waqar Iqbal" the supreme commander of "Al Noora" to give him some assignment of carrying out there jihadist organizations alleged illegal business deal.

Fazal one late morning standing with his back leaning against the big tree, and observing the men and women taking combative action training, a young blonde woman approaches Fazal wearing a smile, she comes close to Fazal and says, hi, friend, why are you standing alone? Fazal acknowledges the gesture of the young lady, says, hi, I'm waiting for "Waqar" one of the head of "Al Noora jihadist group" to assign me some work until than I'm simply spending my time in this camp observing others taking combative and suicide bomb explosion training.

The young girl introduces herself as "Hala," Fazal introduces himself and tells her, I'm Fazal khan Bangash from Afghanistan, Hala reacts, oh, you are an Afghan, Fazal smiles, yes, I am, Fazal ask Hala, you look to me like you are an European, am I right, Hala confirms, yes, you've guessed it right.

Hala tells, I'm a full time member of the jihadist group "Al Noora," Hala add, I'm associated with "Al Noora" jihadist group for the 3 years, I'm in charge of storing and maintaining arms ammunition and explosive, plus I also give training to new jihadist recruit.

Hala and Fazal pleasantly and cordially converse, Fazal in the midst of conversation gauge Hala's mood than ask her, what brought you here? How did you became part of this jihadist world, whom outside world consider as inhuman terrorist? Hala becomes emotional, and replies, I'm a convert, I'm originally from France, Fazal acknowledges her, ok, Hala add, my life is a very sordid tale.

Fazal says, oh, sorry, I don't mean to hurt you, Hala says, no its ok, you are a nice man, listen to my story, Fazal nods his head, Hala says, I'd very turbulent childhood, I'm originally from French city "Rennes," my birth name is Amelia Moreau, we are three siblings, my father deserted my mother and ran away when I was just 8 years of age, I'm the youngest child, my mother as a single mom had to bear great pain in bring us up.

My mother too passed away when I was just 16 years of age, my elder brother also left us two sister alone and went away to Canada, my only sister found a man and went away, I don't know where she went with the man and where and which part of the world is she in right now.

Hala continues, I started doing some odd job in my hometown Rennes, once, while I was working at a Bar, as a waitress, my age was 20 years, one day while commuting in train, a Muslim man occupied an empty seat next to me, and he started talking to me, I as well consider him to be a good man, his approach was very humble, hence I also started conversing with him.

During the course of the conversation he really impressed me by his vocabulary, that man brought up the topic of religion, and he started explaining me all about Islam is great detail, finally our destination arrive, coincidently mine as well as his destination were the same, so we both got off from the train, before parting ways he left his contact Number with me, more so, that Muslim man opened his bag and handed me one book and few loose pages with religious literature printed on it.

Hala says, I was naïve, I spent nearly two days reading the same religious book and other papers with Islamic literature typed on it, now to cut long story short, I got so impressed with the Islamic teachings, that, I approached that same Islamic man whom I'd met in train, when I met him he explained to me more about Islam, Hala add, I was swoon with that man and his Islamic teaching, than what happen is that in my hometown itself I converted to Islam, and that Islamic man convinced me how honourable will it be for me to serve religious purpose, how beneficial will it be and it will take me close and closer to "Divine" if I voluntarily become a Fedayeen (sacrifice life for religion), Hala says, I agreed to his suggestion, and he arranged my induction is this Al Noora jihadist organization.

Hala tells to Fazal, this was my brief life story, Fazal takes a deep breath and says, “Heart Rending” my thoughts are with you, Fazal add, you basically have become a victim of circumstances.

Hala says, each of us have our own destiny, we have to learn to be complacent with what we are, as we are made to be what we are today, Fazal replies, I can’t agree with you more than what you’ve just said, yes, our life has got a lot to do with our destiny.

Hala ask Fazal, what has brought you here to this jihadist training camp? Fazal replies, I’m here by my own choice, Hala ponders than ask, but, why? Fazal smirks and elucidates, I want to become a Rich and powerful person, I’m in this camp to gain wealth and power, but more important is that I want give a new dimension to my life, I want to make my life purposeful, I’m not a type of person who like to live a very stereotyped life.

Hala comments, ok, so, you want to live an action pack life, is that, what you are craving for? Fazal replies, yes, you’ve understood me correct.

Hala expresses her happiness, I’m so happy to have met you and spoke to you, today is the first time, I’ve open up and spoke my heart and mind out to someone, Hala add, “Fazal” you are different person all together, Hala ask, will you become my friend? Fazal smiles, nods his head, yes, Hala replies, thank you, but, my English is not good, Hala says, your English is very good, do all Afghans speak good English like you? Fazal answers, Thank you, well not many, but, fair bit of Afghans are good with the English language and English vocabulary, Fazal add, about my English language speaking quality, well, I’ve mastered my English language, because I spend considerable time reading English literature and watching documentaries on TV.

Hala comprehends, oh, that's good, Fazal points his finger in direction of his tent and shows Hala his tent and tells her, that is the tent where I'm accommodated, Hala ask, who all are there in your family? Fazal replies, we live in joint family, my family consist of my mother, brother, two sisters, and I've a third sister "Heena" who apparently is also my stepsister as well as my stepdaughter and my beautiful wife "Yalda" who is currently expecting a child.

Hala laughs and says, ok, buddy, it's enough for the time being, I'll not ask you anything more, you provided me so much information about yourself and your family, Fazal laughs, hah, hah, hah, always pleasure meeting you and talking to you, Hala tells, ok, I've to join the camp and start my work, I'll be in touch with you, Fazal says, ok.

Chapter 12

After simply waiting and doing nothing in the "Al Noora jihadist" training camp for nearly three long weeks.

Fazal is summoned by the head of Al Noora "Waqar Iqbal" in his office room, Fazal walks up to meet his immediate boss "Waqar" in his private room.

Waqar welcomes Fazal in his room, ask him, so, tell me young man, how's you been all these days in this jihadist training camp? Fazal smirks than replies, oh, sir, I'm frustrated, it's been lonely feeling for me in the training camp without any work, Waqar nods his head, acknowledges the fact, says, ok, I will tell you, as in, why I couldn't assign you any work up till now, but, not anymore, you'll not have to wait, I've manage to convince my other senior colleagues and they've agreed and permitted me to entrust work responsibility to you.

Waqar words enraptures Fazal and brings smile on his face.

Waqar elucidates, Fazal painstakingly listens, Waqar says, normally we don't trust a new recruit and don't assign them any significantly important and perilous responsibility, Waqar adds, you are an exception, hence, I took enormous pain to convince my senior colleagues to bestow upon you a very crucial responsibility, Fazal ask, what? Waqar comments, as you know and I've also told you the other day that our Jihadist organization needs lots of money for us to meet our working capital requirements, our organization expenses are bulging like any other businesses, both due to inflation as well as ever so increasing significant risk of being decimated by various government forces, we have to keep modernizing our combative strength and for that we have to constantly keep upgrading our own combative hardware and software with modern tech arms and computer software for different purposes.

Fazal acknowledges, says, yes, I know this very well, Waqar says, our jihadist organization generates financial resources by indulging in illegal sleazy trades, like Drugs smuggling, illegal Betting Match Fixing etc, Fazal nods his head, yes, sir, I know this very well.

Waqar says, than listen what work I have for you, it's very dangerous, Fazal responses, don't bother, I'm here to play with fire, I have immense appetite for taking risk, Waqar assertively compliments Fazal, this is why I've immense faith in you, I know it that you'll never let me down, Fazal smiles, Thank you, tell me the work.

Waqar elaborates, you'll have to travel all the way to Morocco, you have to visit a very beautiful and artistic Moroccan city of "Casablanca," I'll provide every possible details in terms of contact numbers names and addresses.

Fazal queries, ok, so, what I have to do in Moroccan city of Casablanca? Waqar says, there in Casablanca you have to meet a man whose name is "Mohammed Hamza," he "Mohammed Hamza" will hand you few huge packets and those packets will be containing in it huge quantity of Hashish and Cocaine, Fazal bit jittery but puts up brave face, he ask Waqar, what I have to do then? Waqar explains, he "Mohammed Hamza" will than introduce you to a local man in Casablanca, you'll than have to accompany that unknown person, along with that man you'll have to load the packets of Hashish and Cocaine in to a small speed boat, and then that man will steer the speed boat across the Mediterranean sea to the Portugal city of Setubal.

In Portugal city of "Setubal" on the coast itself present will be our European agent standing and waiting for you, his name is "Mir Aslam Jaan," Waqar says, you have to hand him packets containing Hashish and Cocaine to Mir Aslam, that's it and then in the same speed boat you have to return back to Moroccan city of "Casablanca," and from Casablanca return back here to this jungles of Somalia.

Fazal assures Waqar, your work will be done, have faith in me there won't be any error from my side, Fazal ask, when do I have to leave on this adventure? Waqar says, after three days, Waqar add, I have full faith in you and your skills, Waqar says to Fazal, you have to start your journey to Morocco after 3 days, and for the next 2 days you will have to take rigorous combative arms and explosive training.

Waqar also conveys to Fazal, once you complete the deal of supplying Hashish and Cocaine across the Mediterranean Sea, you get "US Dollar 20,000" cash prize, Fazal response, Thank you, "US$ 20,000" is quite an fetching amount, Waqar laughs, yes, once your first deal is completed successfully, I'll give you even more fetching deals, I'll throw at you lucrative earning opportunity.

Waqar says, now final thing let me explain to you, the travelling itinerary, Waqar explains, your journey from this jihadist training camp will start by road, Waqar says to Fazal, you'll be driven by road from here to Kenyan capital city of "Nairobi," from Nairobi you'll board a flight and reach Moroccan city of "Casablanca," where you have to meet our agent "Mohammed Hamza," and what happens from there on I've already explained that to you.

Fazal replies, ok, sir, Thank you, I've imbibe everything you've briefed me about, Waqar wishes Fazal good luck and concludes the meeting.

Fazal with mounting horror walks back to his tent, later Fazal eats a quite dinner, and returns back inside his tent, Fazal recumbent on bed, vividly things, how dangerous terrain I'm above to enter, should I back off or should ignore the immanent risk and go ahead on the perilous mission, Fazal also thinks, back home in Kabul I've my beautiful wife who's expecting my child, Fazal a brave man shrugs off his fear and says to himself, once I have taken a step forward there's no question of me having a second thought I'm ready to face any consequences.

The dawn breaks out, Fazal is woken up early morning, as he has to start his combative training, and guess, what? Waqar has given a responsibility to train Fazal to one man whose name is Majid, but that's not all, he has also appointed "Miss Hala" a Fazal's favourite in the camp to train him.

Hala happily approaches Fazal and tells him, I have been given responsibility to train you, I will train you and teach you how to operate arms and ammunition like guns like “AK47” and small revolvers and my other colleague Majid will train you and brief you about the use and defensive part of explosive devises.

Fazal says to Hala, what a nice coincident I’m thankful to our immediate boss “Waqar Iqbal” to have appointed you as my trainer, Hala smiles and replies, it’s my honour and pleasure to train an intrepid and intellectual man like you, Fazal says, please don’t flatter today I’m your student, hence treat me like your student and I’ll treat you like my master, Hala says, done, come let us start training.

Fazal gets intense and comprehensive training from Hala and Majid, Fazal a quick learner doesn’t waste enough time he quickly picks up from the tips and guidance as in how to use heavy machine guns, how to operate AK47 guns, also Majid teaches Fazal how to explode hand grenades and how to detonate bombs, how to save ourselves from being attack.

After two days of rigorous combative training, at the end of the second day in the evening, Fazal spends few moments with Hala, Fazal tells Hala, tomorrow early morning my journey commence, I’m embarking on a perilous journey, Hala becomes emotional, she says, I’ll pray that you return back un harm, Hala add, you mean a lot to me please be careful, Fazal glances at Hala top to bottom, says, my friend we are part and parcel of dangerous intimate world, we survive under the seedy and belly of underworld, we need to stay a step ahead of law, and we are constantly expose to potential risk all the time, Hala comprehends Fazal, but, we also have the right to survive, Fazal assures Hala, don’t worry about me, I’ll return back un harm from my perilous journey, Hala responses, I’ll wait for you, Fazal returns back to his tent and doze off to sleep.

Next Morning, Fazal is requested to get ready, and be prepare to live from the jihadist camp before the dawn breaks, Fazal quickly packs his bags, and loads his luggage in a Car, Fazal accompanied by two other Al Noora jihadist group Men, one of them is diver and other is accompanying Fazal to prepare the ground work for Fazal to complete his deal of supplying Narcotics across the Mediterranean sea.

Fazal's journey has started the car breaks through the dangerous African landscape, Fazal unperturbed by any potential unintended consequence sitting in the window seat enjoys the view of great African countryside panoramic view.

Fazal reaches Kenyan city of "Nairobi," Fazal has to spend one night in Nairobi, Fazal spends a night in Nairobi hotel and next morning he takes a flight from Nairobi international airport and goes to Moroccan city of "Casablanca."

In this beautiful picturesque city of Casablanca, Fazal admires the artistic look of historic city of Casablanca, but, Fazal khan Bangash is in casablanca not to admire its beauty but to complete an intimate assignment, Fazal establishes contact with his henchman "Mohammed Hamza," Mr Hamza sitting in a room booked in five star hotel, he calls Fazal over to meet him in the hotel room, Fazal confident swagger his way through the hotel lobby and walks upstairs to meet Mohammed Hamza at his room.

Mohammed Hamza welcomes Fazal without wasting anytime he hands him four big boxes contains Hashish and Cocaine to Fazal.

Fazal takes delivery of Hashish and Cocaine from Mohammed Hamza, Mr Hamza provides Fazal to big suitcase for him to put those four boxes, Fazal carefully puts the four boxes containing Hashish and Cocaine, two boxes each in two bags, ensures the bag is properly packed.

Mohammed Hamza than makes a phone call and request a gentleman to come over to meet him in his room right away, the gentleman from the other side speaking to Mr Hamza confirms he'll be at his hotel room in few minutes.

Few moments later a man arrives to meet Mohammed Hamza in his room, Mr Hamza introduces the gentleman to waiting Fazal as "Tony," Mohammed Hamza tells Fazal, he is "Tony" and he'll accompany you and he will ride the speed boat and take you across the Mediterranean Sea, Fazal greets "Tony" with a warm handshake, Tony ask Fazal, so, buddy, are you ready to accompany me, we both have together embark on most perilous journey across the Mediterranean Sea, Mr Hamza puts his hand on Fazal's shoulder and ask him, are you aware that you have to cross the international sea water, and in the sea water will be the presence of various country police and navy forces patrolling the water.

Fazal after listening to both "Tony and Mr Hamza" comments, "gracious man obtains dignity and aggressive man obtains wealth," I'm an aggressive man, I've learnt to play with fire from the word go in my mother's womb itself, hence nothing in this world fears me.

Mohammed Hamza and Tony, face enlightens listening to Fazal's brave comments, Mr Hamza compliments Fazal with big hug and kisses his forehead and says, you are brave and assiduous man, and I like brave hearted man like you.

Tony tells Fazal, come buddy, let's move now, Fazal accompanied with Tony leaves the hotel and drives to an isolated coastal area in the remote region on the outskirt of Casablanca, Tony ask Fazal to unload his bags and load them in the speedboat, Fazal with the help of Tony and one of "Tony's" acquaintance loads two heavy bags containing Hashish and Cocaine in the speedboat.

Tony starts the boat, and cutting the water waves at great speed "Tony" controlling the steering, speeds his speedboat, on the way they spots several Naval Ships patrolling the most sensitive water zone in the Mediterranean Sea.

Fazal and Tony dodges the policing ships patrolling the zone, and safely reaches their destination which is a Portugal costal town city of "Setubal," Tony spots "Al Noora jihadist group" European agent "Mir Aslam Jaan" standing in disguise, Tony tells Fazal, unload the bags from the ship, Fazal unloads the bags from the speedboat, Mir Aslam Jaan approaches Fazal, Fazal ask Mir Aslam Jaan to confirm code word for recognition, Aslam confirms the code word, Fazal satisfied he's the right man, Fazal hands him over the two huge suitcase containing Hashish and Cocaine.

Mir Aslam Jaan Thanks Fazal for delivering him the boxes containing Hashish and Cocaine and now it's the responsibility of Mir Aslam Jaan to take the boxes to the final destination, on his part Fazal khan Bangash a Pashtun from Kabul has completed his assignment successfully.

Tony refuels his speedboat, Fazal gets inside the speedboat and starts his return journey, Fazal returns back to the AL Noora jihadist camp in the jungle of Somalia un harm, much to the delight of Miss Hala who was apparently unduly worried about the safety of her (she has a romantic feeling for Fazal which she's concealing) special friend "Fazal."

Hala approaches Fazal and expresses her satisfaction about him retuning back to the camp un harmed, Fazal as well equally satisfied and happy to be back in the training camp and to meet his new found lady (Fazal as well has passion for Hala and he as well like her is also reticent) friend.

Waqar Iqbal overwhelmingly happy with Fazal the manner in which he completed his first ever deal of supplying Narcotics drugs across the Mediterranean Sea.

Waqar compliments Fazal, says, you very meticulously completed the deal of Supplying Hashish and Cocaine across the sea, I'm proud of you, Fazal responses, I'm grateful to you that you trusted me and gave me an opportunity to carry out intimate trade, Waqar tells Fazal, come over to my room and take your prize money of "US$ Twenty Thousand,"

Fazal gets paid Twenty thousand US Dollars, Waqar throws another offer to Fazal, he tells him now I have full faith in you and your ability to undertake any sort of intimate assignment, Waqar says, I and my other colleagues have observe that you have tremendous fire power, Fazal assertively replies, I'm a person who's born to play with fire.

Waqar says, ok, listen to my other offer for you, Fazal queries, what? Waqar says, you have to go to Cairo an Egyptian capital, Waqar add, you'll have to camp in Cairo for nearly two weeks, Fazal inquires, ok, but, what I have to do for two long weeks in Egypt? Waqar elucidates, you'll have to strike Match Fixing deals, Waqar continues, in next two days, African football league will commence in Egypt, the matches will be played in various Egyptian towns and cities, and you have to base yourself in capital city of Cairo and manage the match fixing of most of those football matches.

Waqar elaborates, in Cairo city you have to contact two of our henchman, they both are reputed sports journalist and are on payroll of my AL Noora jihadist organization, their names are “Bilal Ahmad and other is Habil Mussa,” Waqar says, both Bilal and Habil have unprecedented access to every football team that will be participating in African football league, and both these journalist will fix the matches as we like them to be fixed, as most of the prominent footballers have good rapport with Bilal and Habil and they will be more than willing to throw away games if we throw at them lucrative and engaging Cash offers, Fazal ask Waqar, ok, I’ve understood what these match fixing deals are all about, but any particular instruction for me.

Waqar says to Fazal, I have consulted my other senior colleagues and they have given me there nod, to trust you, hence I’m giving you free hand to use your own desecration, and fix the matches as you think is appropriate, Waqar perspicuously tells Fazal, you will have total freedom to decide on offer price to offer the players, so in consultation with Bilal and Habil you can fix the matches as you think is appropriate, you have a total free hand, Fazal says, ok, done, I’ll ensure that I earn lots of money and contribute that money in the kitty of your “Al Noora jihadist organization,” Waqar reacts, excellent, Waqar tells Fazal, you’ll get 15% commission on the total profit you earn for my Al Noora group thru match fixing, will that be enough for you? Fazal nods his head, yes, 15% commission is a good amount to earn, please bless me that I succeed in striking lucrative Match Fixing deals.

Waqar tells Fazal, you are very proficient and perspicacious young man, I’m convince you’ll succeed in your endeavour, Waqar request Fazal, please ensure you make most of this opportunity and make lots of money for my “Al Noora jihadist group” because we need lots of money as the expenditure of our group activity are rising exponentially, Fazal assures, yes, I’ll resolutely strive to make most of the opportunity, Fazal concludes meeting with Waqar and steps out of his room and walks towards his tent, Fazal meets his friend “Hala” and tells her, he’s going to be away from jihadist camp and will be camping in Egypt for few weeks, Hala wishes Fazal Good luck and tells him, I’ll miss you and will wait for you to return and pray for your success, Fazal gaze at Hala and says, Thank you, even I’ll miss you, but when I come back we’ll spend lot of time together, Hala replies, oh, really, Fazal says, yes.

The day is Saturday, and, Fazal very early in the morning lives the "Al Noora jihadist" camp in the Somalian jungle, and embarks on excursion to Egypt.

Fazal reaches Egypt, he bases himself in upscale luxurious Hotel in Cairo, a suite is booked for Fazal, from where he will manage his illegal betting and match fixing activity.

Fazal without wasting any time of his immediately plunge into huddle, Fazal summons his points men Bilal Ahmad and Habil Mussa to his hotel suite and starts planning Match Fixing deals for the ongoing African Football league, Fazal gets intensely busy discussing and planning Match fixing deal.

Fazal aided by two senior sports journalist Bilal and Habil establishes contact with few of top African footballers agent and few top national teams official and by throwing lucrative offers and goodies, Fazal wins them over and makes them agree to manipulate results of some of the important football matches to be played, the players agents on behalf of the key football players and few top officials of top football team strikes deal with Fazal and agrees to throw away football games.

Fazal khan Bangash meticulously plans Match fixing and comprehensively manages the financial resources, and bets on each of the football matches that he fixes and gets resounding success, Fazal apart from using the money provided to him by the leadership of "Al Noora jihadist organization," Fazal takes the odd risk and dabbles with his own cash as well to bet on the African football leagues matches which fixes with the participating players, Fazal two weeks stays in Egypt proves very lucrative, Fazal thanks Bilal and Habil for cooperating with him and making his first dash with allege betting and match fixing a resounding success, Fazal pays attractive remuneration to both "Bilal and Habil."

Fazal returns back to Somalia, Fazal returns back to "Al Noora jihadist training camp," Fazal has returned triumphant, Fazal made a profit of whopping Forty Million US dollar by betting on African football league matches.

Fazal gets an heroic welcome in the Al Noora camp, by the supreme leader "Waqar Iqbal," Waqar informs Fazal, all my other senior colleagues are sincerely grateful to you, you've done a commendable job, you manage the whole match fixing and betting operation extremely professionally like no one else have done before.

Fazal by proving his proficiency and courage in "wheeling and dealing art," Fazal is entrusted with some more vital responsibility from the bosses of "Al Noora jihadist group."

Fazal plays crucial role in overseeing the nefarious activity of Al Noora jihadist organization, Fazal takes responsibility of haggling out clandestine deals with several "North and Central African government" and the insurgent forces active in North Africa and Arabian peninsula, Fazal at his own risk supplies arms and ammunition to insurgent forces in few African and Arabian country, Fazal also strategically masterminds jihadist militia terrorist attack in many African countries and also secretly helps many African government defeat militancy in their country.

Fazal becomes a pampered boy in the ranks and files of "Al Noora jihadist organization," Fazal starts enjoying special privileges in the jihadist camp, also his friendship with the French convert girl "Hala" flourishes into romance.

Chapter 13

Over five months have passed for Fazal joining the "Al Noora jihadist group" and staying in the bushy jungle of Somalia.

One day Fazal request his friend "Hala" to get inside the Car and come with him on a long drive, Hala always craving to spend time with her dearest friend "Fazal," she lives the work that she's doing and gets inside the Car and tells Fazal, comes lets go on adventure drive, it will be fun, Fazal responses, fun, you said, Hala nods, yes, Fazal says, yes, indeed, fun, we'll have, and this long drive will be adventurous fantasy, Hala says, enough talking now hit the gas.

In the hot blistering heat of Africa, Fazal drives the Car wildly in the jungle, Fazal has come away far from the Al Noora jihadist camp, in the middle of nowhere, Fazal spots an empty dilapidated house in the jungle and there's no one around, Fazal takes the Car of the road into the rugged field, Hala ask Fazal, where are you taking the car? Here there is nothing, Fazal points his finger and tells her, can't you see this old house, Hala retorts, you call this a house, its a broken small abandon villa, what is so interesting in this broken house? That you've brought me here.

Fazal request Hala, please get down from the vehicle I want to have a close look at this house, Hala obliges, ok, Fazal walks inside the dilapidated house, than tells Hala, at the back in the boot of the Car there is a blanket lying, please get it here, we've come over here for picnic, Hala fumes, but gets the blanket and throws it towards Fazal and says, I'm disgusted, why have you stopped the car in middle of nowhere, there is not a single human or even cattle that I can spot over here complete wilderness.

Fazal laughs and comments, you look devastating when you are angry, Hala puts one hand of her on her waist and stares at Fazal, and Fazal stares back at her, Fazal takes his shirt off, Fazal spreads the blanket on the floor of the dilapidated house, and lies down on floor, Fazal tells Hala my libido is high and I'm craving for pleasure, Hala breathes heavily vividly thinks, what should I do?

Hala softly murmurs, you want to have pleasure in this heat, the strong afternoon Sun heat will tear our skin apart, Fazal says, don't bother, I can't wait anymore please, oblige, I have immense love for you, but, Hala smatters, but, but, Fazal says, stop these if's and but's.

Hala reminds Fazal, there is lot of combative hardware in the vehicle, Fazal replies, forget the Hardware and Software remove your underwear.

Hala comments, you really want pleasure, is this your wish today to have intimate fun in this sweltering heat, Fazal replies, yes.

Hala agrees, if this is what your wish, than, I won't disappoint you.

Hala shed inhibition, says, you naughty boy, Hala disrobes herself, and in a broken house with open roof, braving intense Heat, soaking the Sun, Fazal and Hala frivolously indulges in bodily pleasure.

After well over two hours of indulging ferociously in intimate bodily pleasure, Hala separates herself from Fazal, she tells him, I'm profoundly grateful to you today, you've given me the world, you've given me what every girl/woman crave for, I thoroughly enjoyed sex with you.

Fazal keeps quite only stares at Hala, Hala says, I'm very premonitory, Fazal ask, you feeling premonition, but, why? Hala says, we've exceeded our limit, our religion doesn't allow "fornication," I fear there will be repercussion, Fazal shrugs off her fear, we want to have it, we had it, you want to have it, you had it, damn the consequence.

Fazal add, Why fear? Stop talking and thinking on the line of religion, Hala says, you are married and I'm unmarried, Fazal says, our religion permit polygamy, I'll marry you, is that ok, Hala confuse smatter, but, what will happen? Fazal replies I'll marry and accept you.

Hala queries, but your wife, will, she?

Fazal says, when you love someone, it's something, when someone loves you, it's another thing, when you love a person who loves you back, it's everything.

Hala smiles, you are very poetic fellow, Fazal caresses Hala and says, you think so, that I'm poetic, Hala nods her head, Fazal replies, thank you for your compliments.

Fazal says, please dress up, we have to live and reach back to that stupid hell of the place call "Al Noora jihadist camp," Hala tightly hugs Fazal and says, you just said, hell of the place to our "Al Noora jihadist camp," Fazal makes hum, hum sound, Hala add, yes, this jihadist camp is a terror world.

Hala request Fazal, please, if you love me and your intentions are humble than please take me somewhere far away from this terror world, you are my man, Hala emotionally says, I want to live a peaceful life, I want to have children and family, I don't like to be jihadist world, please take me away out from this perilous life, I'm feeling suffocated in this jihadist camp, you are a nice man, and I trust you.

Fazal listens to Hala, than comments, give me few weeks, I will find some way out, Fazal commits his love to Hala, and Hala assures her unflinching support to Fazal, they both return back to "Al Noora jihadist camp.

Next day, Fazal meets his immediate boss "Waqar Iqbal" and tells him that I need to go back home to "Kabul," Waqar ask, but, why? You are doing so fine,

Fazal says, I want to carve a niche for myself, I'll now work on independent basis, I'll keep my ties with your "Al Noora jihadist organization" intact, but, I want to be a free bird, I don't want to be bind with your jihadist group.

Waqar replies, that's fine with me, you can live for your hometown in Afghanistan to Kabul at your will as an when you want to, Fazal with mounting horror ask Waqar, I have a sincere request to make to you, Waqar smiles, ask, what's your request? Please tell me.

Fazal comments, I want to take with me that French convert lady "Hala" along with me, I want to marry her, we both are in love and exceeded our limit, Fazal looks at Waqar and says, I hope you'll understand.

Waqar disagrees, he says to Fazal, only you can go from here alone, because there is no binding between you and my jihadist group the Al Noora, but the French girl can't live this jihadist organization, it's against the rule of our jihadist organization, no ways I'll not let her step out of this jihadist camp.

Fazal pleads, please, allow her to accompany me, allow her to marry me, we both love each other, Waqar says, you fool, you are an intellectual person, don't you know its "Haram" in our religion to "fornicate," don't you know we can kill that French convert woman "Hala" for having sex with a man whom she's not married, she's committed "Adultery."

Fazal convince Waqar, says, you too are by nature a very secular and liberal person, damn this draconian rule of stoning a woman to death, aren't men of our religion indulging in extra marital affairs, aren't men indulging in sodomy with men's, Fazal adds, please, I have tremendous hope from you, please, allow "Hala" to live this jihadist camp with me.

After intense debate and persuasion the chief leader of "Al Noora jihadist group" relents and after consulting his other senior colleagues, Waqar says to Fazal, ok, considering that you've in recent past considerably helped my jihadist group specially with your skill you've helped in shoring up our "Al Noora jihadist group's" cash reserves, hence, showing leniency towards you my senior colleagues and myself have decided to show remorse towards you.

Waqar gives his consent to Fazal to marry Hala if he wants too, and take her away with him.

Fazal falls on the feet of Waqar and thanks him, Fazal says to Waqar, I'm indebted to you, I'll never forget your leniency and generosity you've rendered on me, by freeing my lady love "Hala," Waqar hugs Fazal and says, enjoy yourself, my best wishes to you and "Hala," Waqar add, go ahead and marry Hala and start a new life with her.

Fazal approaches Hala, and breaks the news to her, He says to Hala, my dear, now you are free to move anywhere you like with me, I've got the permission from the "Al Noora jihadist group" "hierarchy" to marry you and take you along with me.

Hala yelps, wow, my love, what a great news you've given me, Hala joyously says, so, now, I'm liberated, now I can start a new life, now we can marry and have our cute children's, Fazal nods his head in agreement, yes, you are liberated, now the two of us will marry and have our own family.

Chapter 14

Fazal and Hala with the consent from the bosses of Al Noora jihadist group and lives the Al Noora jihadist camp situated in the bushy jungle of Somalia.

Fazal with his lady love "Hala" travel to Kenyan coastal town of "Mombasa," Fazal and Hala gets married in a "Nikah Ceremony" a local Kazi (priest) performs ritual to solemnize of "Amelia Moreau alas Hala's" marriage to Pashtun man from Kabul Fazal khan Bangash.

Hala overwhelmingly ecstatic and elated to become wife of Fazal, Hala and Fazal spends leisure time together, enjoy their honeymoon in the upscale beach resort in Mombasa.

Hala ensures that her beloved husband is fully satisfied she plays role of quintessential wife, passionately indulges in wild sex fantasy to emollient Fazal's mind, both Fazal and Hala are happy to be together and happy to be married to each other.

Fazal hugely loaded with cash, cash is now absolute no problem for Fazal, as he has made huge amount of money working for Al Noora jihadist group, Fazal has lots of money to spend on bling.

After spending 2 weeks long honeymoon, it's time for Fazal to get back to life and back to reality, Fazal hires a private charter plane to take his newly Wed bride "Miss Hala" to his real home, his hometown "Kabul," Hala enthusiastic as well to travel with her husband to his home and meet her in-law's.

Fazal and Hala boards the private plane and embarks on excursion and flies to Kabul.

With mounting unease Fazal hires a private Taxi from outside to Kabul airport and heads towards his house, Fazal a bit jittery wonders how are my family is going to react when they will see wannabe "my second wife' Hala," he also thinks and worries as in, what will be the reaction of my first wife "Yalda" how will she response to when she sees me accompanied with my second wife? Hala sits tight in the vehicle hold hands of Fazal and seeing the sight of arguably the most dangerous city in the world "Kabul city."

The private Taxi reaches the home of Fazal, and Fazal has returned home after well over 6 months.

Fazal's younger sisters Firdoz, Zarine with his stepsister and stepdaughter Heena, spots Fazal arrive and the three sisters loudly yells they shout our brother has arrived and comes running out of the house, Fazal's sisters "Firdoz and Zarine" in excitement hugs and kisses Fazal and expresses there pleasure upon seeing their brother "Fazal" after long time, Fazal carries the youngest of his sister "Heena" in his hand and kisses all three of his sisters.

Firdoz queries, "Brother" who is this beautiful women? Come with you, Fazal answers, her name is "Hala, Firdoz nods her head, Fazal tells his sisters, she is "Hala" and she has come to stay with us, Fazal's sister Zarine approaches Hala and holds her hand and says, she is so nice looking I'm so happy that you will be staying with us.

Hala becomes emotional she greets each of Fazal three sisters, Hala exchanges pleasantries with Fazal sisters and her sister-in-laws.

Fazal and Hala moves inside the house, Fazal first encounters his mother who's sitting in the living room, Fazal hugs his mother and now his first wife emerges out of her room, Fazal has paid surprised visit back home, he didn't give any prior information to his family over the phone or through any correspondence.

Yalda greets her husband with "As-Salamu-Alaykum," Fazal replies back to Yalda "Walay-Kum-As-Salam," Hala is standing in the background holding hands of her two young sis-in-law "Firdoz and Zarine."

Fazal's mother "Farida" queries, referring to "Hala" who is this European woman come along with you and why is she standing far away from us in the doorstep, request her to come in and sit here in the living room.

Hala donning Blue Denim Jeans and Denim shirt but with keeping the Afghan tradition she's clad in chador and head scarf, Fazal request Hala to come closer to his mother, Farida ask her son "Fazal" you haven't answer my question, who is this woman?

Fazal sheepishly first stares at his first wife than glances at his mother, Fazal gathers courage and tells his mother, mamma, she is "Hala" and I met her in Africa and we fell in love and have got married.

Fazal's mother "Farida" reacts furiously, she says, my son, do you have any shame left with you, you've married this Firang (means blonde European woman), how dare you do this, don't you know, aren't you aware that your wife "Yalda" is pregnant with your child.

Yalda most discerning, Yalda heavily pregnant, she calms down her mother-in-law and she approaches her co-wife "Hala" and sits next to her, Yalda displays her solidarity and she hugs and kisses "Hala," and Hala in turn hugs Yalda and weeps and says, please, pardon me, I've butt in to your life, Yalda appreciates Hala's looks, Yalda tells her mother-in-law "Farida" isn't she (Hala) amazing beauty, Yalda says, mamma, we must respect Hala and accept her as member of our family.

Yalda tells her husband "Fazal" congratulation I appreciate your choice, Fazal replies, Yalda I'm sorry, Yalda strikes instant chord with her co-wife "Hala."

Fazal's mother as well mellows down and embraces her new daughter-in-law "Hala," it becomes a happy family union.

Everything falls in place for Fazal, this is the most pivotal moment in Fazal khan Bangash life.

Hala blends herself well with the other family members of her husband's family, Yalda is particularly happy with her co-wife "Hala" as they both jell well, and Fazal is happy and he's on top of the world with two amazingly beautiful women in his life as his wife.

Few weeks of staying together in perfect union, one day, Fazal tells his mother, mamma, I want you and both my sisters "Firdoz and Zarine" to go and settle down in another country, a country where there is peace and harmony and more important where the society is free and liberal, Fazal further adds, I want my elder brother "Karmal" as well to accompany you and he live his studies in Lahore and join you and both my sisters and move out of this region.

Fazal's mother questions his wisdom behind sending them away from their homeland, Fazal replies, mamma, you know, I'm die heart family man, and I'd given commitment to "Daddy" that in his absence y'all will become my responsibility and your safety and security is my concern.

Fazal's mother "Farida" ask, but, what about your safety and the safety of your two wives and kids? Fazal replies, mamma, don't bother about me and you need not have any concern with regards to the safety of my wives and myself.

Fazal elucidates, mamma, I have a plan, I work as per plan, for the time being you live with my other siblings to the safe harbour, Fazal add, when time will be conducive and once I accomplished my objectives achieve my goal, I too along with my wives and kids join y'all and then we all stay together, Fazal continues, mamma, for now, you start packing stuff and get Karmal and both sisters Firdoz and Zarine ready, and be ready to move on.

Fazal's mother "Farida," ask, ok, but, where do we all go? Where are you planning or intending to send us all? Fazal replies, mamma, Australian city of Perth, this city Perth is a beautiful city and y'all will thoroughly enjoy staying in this great Australian city of Perth, far away from this highly conservative and outrageously insular Afghan civil society.

All three of my sibling can pursue their further studies in Perth and I want my sibling to be "liberal, secular and modern."

Farida pleads Fazal to reconsider his decision, Fazal retorts, mamma, my decisions are never roll backed, I still have lots of job at my hand, Fazal tells his mother, mamma, all arrangement of yours along with my three other siblings transition has been made, money is not a problem, rest assure.

Fazal's mother and particularly both his sisters "Firdoz and Zarine" not particularly happy but falls in line, Fazal's mother realize that her son is doing whatever he's doing for the betterment of the family.

Fazal's mother his elder brother "Karmal" and his two sisters "Firdoz and Zarine" departs for good from their homeland Afghanistan.

Fazal rejoices with his 2 elegant and submissive wives, while Yalda is heavily pregnant just few weeks are left for the delivery of her first child, hence the onus is on Fazal's second wife "Hala" to entertain him, Hala does everything she can to make her husband happy, Hala ensures her husband "Fazal" is well entertained and has enough of bodily pleasure.

With lots of pleasure and indulgence finally the stork visits "Hala," Hala becomes pregnant with Fazal's child, Fazal is ecstatic that his second wife's pregnant as well.

One day in the afternoon, Fazal's first wife "Yalda" experiences intense labour pain, Fazal and Hala helps Yalda and rushes her to the nearby nursing home, Fazal with mix feeling waits for the delivery to happen.

Yalda's brings in the world, what's apparently hers and Fazal's first love their first child, the first person to take the child in hand after Yalda is her co-wife "Hala" who's ecstatic and she congratulates both Yalda and her husband "Fazal."

Few moments later Yalda says to Fazal, my husband thank you, hope you're happy with me delivering our first child, Fazal nods his head, Hala kisses Yalda than she kisses Fazal and ask them, have y'all thought of any good name of your new born child.

Fazal takes his new born daughter in his hand tows her, Yalda ask Fazal, what name should we give our "baby"? Fazal glances at his daughter and then stares at both his wives and says, I am naming my daughter, Hala passionately ask, what name you've thought of? Fazal comments, we'll call our new born "baby girl," "Nagma," Fazal says, yes, Nagma is the name of my daughter.

Fazal has become a proud father in addition to his first combine relation of both "stepdaughter as stepsister" "Heena," Fazal is now father of girl child "Nagma."

Yalda returns home from nursing home after few days stay, Hala her co-wife is very discerning woman, she takes over the responsibility of home, as well as provides unsolicited support to her senior co-wife "Yalda" and her new born daughter "Nagma."

Chapter 16

After spending few months at home sorting out his families and personal issues and after lots of pleasure and happiness of becoming father "Fazal khan Bangash has to make fresh new moves.

Fazal ensures everything is in order on home front, both his wives have settled down all personal issues amicably sorted out.

Fazal calls both his wives for discussion, Yalda ask, my husband hope everything is fine, why have you called both of us? Hala as well queries, what's the matter? Fazal tells both his wives, I have to embark on a journey, tomorrow morning I'll live on my excursion, first I'll travel to Pakistani city of "Lahore" and then depending on the outcome of my meeting with a "power broker" (liaise) I may have to travel even further far away from Pakistan.

Yalda inquires, how long will be your excursion? When can we expect you to return home? Fazal replies, I'm clueless, at this point I've no firm answer for your query, Hala understands he's setting himself on a perilous mission, Hala says, ok, honey, we'll wait for you, all our best wishes to you, Fazal says, thank you, to both of for being considerate.

Fazal spends rest of the day playing with his daughters "Nagma and stepdaughter Heena," later Fazal packs his bags and keeps himself ready to proceed on his excursion.

The dawn break out, Fazal eats early breakfast, Fazal exchanges pleasantries with his wives and loves his daughters and embarks on the journey to Lahore.

Fazal reaches the Pakistani city of "Lahore," in Lahore's plush Five Star hotel a suite is booked for Fazal.

Fazal check-in the hotel occupies Room a "luxurious Suite," Fazal settles down in his hotel room.

Late afternoon a stunning socialite an exquisitely beautiful woman arrives to meet Fazal, and Fazal graciously and perkily greets that beautiful lady and her name is "Afshan khan."

Afshan is a Pakistan based TV journalist, she's a good blend of beauty with brain, but she's also cunning and floozy, but above all Afshan is a power broker, she indulges in sly deals between interested parties and the deals which are nefarious in nature.

Fazal and Afshan both realizing the fact that how so important both are for each other hence both behave obsequiously with each other.

Fazal and Afshan starts conversation with exchanging pleasantries, after small talk, Fazal tells Afshan, shall we come to the point shall talk business, Afshan with sulky expression replies, oh, my dear, so soon, she looks at her watch, I've just arrived in your room to meet you, Afshan add, how mean of you, you are in such desperate hurry to talk business with me and chase me out of your beautiful hotel room soon.

Fazal sheepishly reacts, oh, no, friend, don't misunderstand me, I didn't mean what you are thinking, Afshan responses, sweetie, how rude you can be, I say you men's, you are addressing me, a beautiful young woman like me as "friend."

Fazal smiles and comments, what's wrong, in me addressing you as "friend," Afshan vociferates, I'm addressing you by calling you "sweetie and handsome," and you, how boring.

Fazal says, you "Afshan" you're a dazzling woman, to meet a woman as volatile like you particularly in this part of the world where the people are so outrageously conservative, Afshan replies, is this the compliment for me or criticism, Fazal replies, you may have your own conclusion if any, I've merely described you the way I thought you are as a person.

Afshan comments, you said about me I'm a dazzling and volatile woman, well if you think so maybe that's perhaps the reason men's run away from me as if I'm 440volts power current.

Afshan ask Fazal, with your permission may I get a bit personal and more casual with you, Fazal nods, how can I ever say "No" to you, Fazal sarcastically add, you are free to get personal or "overcome," sweetheart.

Afshan ecstatic, you addressed me as "sweetheart" oh, darling I'm so overwhelm, Afshan gets up from her chair she's sitting on and passionately comes closer to Fazal who is sitting on the sofa, Afshan passionately kisses Fazal on both his cheeks, she enthusiastically rubs her cheeks with Fazal's cheeks and puts her arm around Fazal and sits tightly close to him.

Afshan queries, I've learnt from my sources that while you were working with "Al Noora jihadist organization" in the jungles of Somalia you fell in love with a French woman and have married her since, darling, am I right? Fazal says, yes, indeed, you've got this information which is correct.

Afshan reacts, how mean, you fell in love while you were married to a woman, because my sources have also told me that the French girl whom you married is your second wife, your first wife is a beautiful afghan woman.

Fazal scratches his head than frowns, he says, gosh, you are rigorously grilling me, Afshan retorts, we woman have to be aggressive, Fazal replies, I love aggressive woman.

Afshan how nice of you love, that's why I'm behaving aggressively with you so that you love me, Fazal jokingly says, you are a "Lamia," Afshan furiously reacts, you told me I'm like a "Lamia," Fazal replies, yes, my beautiful Lamia.

Afshan mellows down, honey, I'm just kidding, with you love, you are such an adorable man, Fazal says, Thank you, Afshan says, you rude man, please, I warn you don't take my gesture for granted.

Fazal reaffirms, you "Lamia" I am going to swallow you, Afshan replies, how romantic, but before that tell me, how does it feel to you to be married to two young beautiful woman at the same time.

Afshan continues asking, it must fascinating for you right, lots of pleasure fun wild fantasy, oh, gosh, how lucky a person can be I can just imagine, but sadly, why I'm I not so fortunate my love life never blossomed.

Fazal renders a juicy kiss to Afshan and answers, yes, I'm considering myself lucky, many society and cultures consider polygamy as taboo or stigma, but, I'm an eccentric man, I like living my life on my own terms, Afshan passionately ask Fazal, sweetie please unravel some more facts about your life, I'm finding your true life story very romantic and excited.

Fazal obliges and disclose more information about himself to ever so desperate "Afshan khan," Fazal add, both my wives "Yalda and Hala" are young sexy and very submissive wives, I have my hands full so far as love is concern both my wives passionately loves me admires me and cares for me.

Afshan gets up from the sofa, pours water in a glass and drinks two full glasses of water, Fazal opens the refrigerator and removes two "Cans of Beer," Fazal ask, young lady, would you like to have a glass or two of Beer, Afshan nods her head, says, yes, honey, I desperately need to dope to soothe my mind.

Afshan and Fazal raises toast for the evening, after drinking few sips of Beer, Fazal jokingly tells Afshan, love, you've asked me lot about myself, and I obliged by telling you lot about my family life. The evening has just started and we have to spend many more hours together in this hotel suite, hence let me listen to something about your life.

Afshan listens to Fazal and drinks the entire Beer that's left in the glass, she request Fazal for second helping of Beer, Fazal pours another large Can of Beer in the empty glass of Afshan.

Afshan starts by saying, honey as much happiness and as much blissful your life is that much boring and disappointed is or has been my life.

Fazal queries, you're an amazing woman, how is it the you've not learn the art of keeping your own life exciting, Afshan says, we can't be perfect in every department hence the life goes this way that an individual may be extremely intelligent in one aspect of life but an absolute "Zero" with many more aspect of life, hence we find so many people in the world who keep creeping about their pain, Afshan add, hence my life's real story is a sordid Tale.

Afshan elaborates, Fazal listens to Afshan with eyes wide open, Afshan says, I have been married twice in my life, and both my marriage faltered.

Fazal empathize, how sad, what happen? Afshan continues conversation, my first marriage was to a man whom I knew from my childhood his name was "Arif," both of us were also family friends, Afshan add, both Arif and myself grew together we were together in same school and also for the first few years we studied in the same college, till the time we both decided to choose different career option, he went on to study Law while I enrol myself in journalism.

In between sipping Beer Afshan further says, after the both of us completed our studies and started working, when my age was 24 years I got married to my childhood love "Arif," Afshan tells, like every woman even I was of the belief that getting married is an ultimate happiness, I had lots of dream, and getting married to a man whom I so passionately loved all my life, when I got married to him I considered myself to be the luckiest woman.

Fazal ask, than, what happen? Afshan replies, what happen after I got married to my childhood sweetheart was nothing but pain, My stupid husband started treating my body like his own property, he had nothing else to do, Afshan comments, "come on" this men's should realize that we woman also need a space to live, but this man who was my than husband use to perennially bother me, umpteen time in a day he use to call me, whether from his office or otherwise and disturb me, when he use to close to me, he use to constantly ask and demand his marital privileges, he use to keep tickling me, pinching me, spank me he use fondle with my tits ask me to have sex at odd time.

Afshan elucidates, because of my husband "Arif's" bad bedroom etiquettes I started feeling suffocated in the relationship, and finally after three years in relationship through mutual understanding we divorced and that's how my first marriage fell apart.

Fazal again empathizes, darling my heart goes out for you, Afshan gives a passionate tight hug and renders few kisses to Fazal than says, sweetie, now quickly listen what happen to my second marriage.

Fazal smirks, ok, love lets listen, Afshan elaborates, after my first marriage ended on the bitter note, I was single for next three years, even though in between I did had couple of flings, Fazal makes hum sound, Afshan vociferates, of course, I'm a woman I have feeling and I as well need bodily pleasure, Fazal nods his head, of course, woman as well needs pleasure, Afshan comments, oh, darling how considerate of you, you understand woman's feeling rather to well.

Fazal ask, ok, than, what happen? Afshan add, at our common friend birthday bash I happen to meet a young hunk, I mean to say a man who was incredibly handsome, wow I must say, he was so good looking that I immediately fell for him, he too was from this same city Lahore and he was a successful businessman, his name was "Fawad."

Afshan add, after meeting "Fawad" I once again thought that my life will become complete once I tie knot with this handsome rich businessman, even though he was a divorcee but so was I, we both divorcee thought that since we've both suffered the pain and been through agonizing spell in our life, Afshan add, Fawad and I thought learning from our past mistake we would prove to be quintessential husband and wife and a dotting couple.

Afshan further says, we both got married here in Lahore in a small ceremony, Afshan says, now listen to the fun, Fazal responses, how interesting please tell what happen? I'm curious, Afshan gives juicy kiss to Fazal and says to him, my second husband was a real "Nitwit," he was such frigid fellow, his libido use to never rise, he never use to arouse sexually, he use to spend most of his time away from home, use to travel a lot.

Afshan elaborates, when in bedroom, whenever he use to see me nude he use to shudder emotionally, when I use to spread my legs and make advances at him, when I passionately use to call him near me to suck in me, that arse use literally faint, Afshan holds her head in disgust and tells Fazal, my second marriage could last for only one year, fed of his behaviour I decided to call it quits, hence my second marriage as well was terminated, or to says my second marriage proved even bigger disappointment than my first marriage.

Fazal tilts his head down and shows it to Afshan, looks we've finished "6 Cans of Beer each" listening to your life story, Afshan sufficiently intoxicated, says, don't bemoan, it's you who were curious to know my life story.

Fazal calls hotel room service orders dinner, after dinner, Afshan gets in a seductive mood, she says to Fazal, the onus is on you to make my day, Fazal jokes, it night babes, Afshan says, you creep, my mood has sucked telling you my life story of my two failed marriage.

Fazal ask, what do you need out of me? Afshan replies, pleasure, Fazal replies, pleasure with pleasure, my love, Afshan disrobes herself, Fazal sees Afshan standing in front of him in her lingerie, Fazal comments, wow, some lingerie's are exquisitely design to have erotic effect.

Afshan donning incredibly seductive lingerie, she says, do you know many men's like to steal woman's under garments and store it they say they like the scent of women's lingerie, Fazal comments, how the hell you get such ridiculous inside out stories, Afshan replies, don't you know I'm a journalist by profession, beside I'm twice married and twice divorce and apart several flings that I've had.

Fazal craving for pleasure says, damn your profession and my profession it's time for indulgences, "raffish" Afshan and "Pashtun hunk" Fazal khan Bangash passionately indulges with raunchy "Afshan khan."

The night passes by, Afshan and Fazal thoroughly enjoys there activity.

The dawn breaks out, it's time to wake up, Afshan and Fazal wakes up, both compliment and Thanks each other for the overnight fun and pleasure.

After breakfast it's time to talk real business.

Afshan khan occupies her seats, she lights a cigarette takes few drags, and tells Fazal who's sitting across the table, Afshan begins by saying, I've a deal for you and I'm sure you'll find the deal interesting to work on.

Fazal nods his head, ask Afshan to elaborate, says, I'd gone to India last month, I was in Indian capital city of "New Delhi" in regards to my work, Afshan adds,

I had gone to "New Delhi" to attend a press conference and also prepare documentary on lifestyle of rural India.

Afshan continues, during my stay in the Indian Capital, through a common friend, I met my Indian counterpart who's a renown Indian journalist and he also works for private TV News channel as an News Anchor and his name is "Sudhir Singh," Afshan add, this gentleman "Sudhir Singh" and I spent considerable time together discussing wide range of topic as we both have lots of common interest.

Fazal ask, ok, tell me, what's there for me? Afshan smirks and comments, darling, have patients, I'm coming to the point, Fazal replies, you are advising me to have patients, how much more patients? am I supposed to have I've damn spend a full night waiting to listen from you as to what is that intimate deal that you are trying to broker with me, Afshan reacts, kisses Fazal on both his cheeks and says, ok, my honey, please forgive me but I won't take more time of yours, I promise I'll be quick, Fazal acknowledges, its, ok, I have patients.

Afshan says, this gentleman the Indian journalist is also a "liaise" and he is currently visiting Pakistan and he is very much in this town "Lahore" itself.

Afshan explains, I have no clue as in, what this Indian journalist fellow has to offer, but he has requested me to arrange a meeting with a person who has considerable influence and clout in the Islamic terror world, Afshan says, hence, I have contact you, this journalist "Sudhir" is staying in the hotel which is just next to this hotel where we are right now.

Afshan tell Fazal, the nature of the deal obviously will potentially be aggressive and destructive, and if you are interested I can arrange a meeting between you and the visiting Indian journalist later today late night at a neutral venue.

Fazal frowns and agrees, yes, I'll be interested to meet this Indian journalist "Sudhir Singh" and listen to him and see what he has to offer me? Further in regards to your comments, as in, the deal will be "aggressive and destructive" in nature, Fazal laughs and says, in the outrageously menacing and sleazy profession that I'm in every damn deals are supposed to be destructive in nature, but.

Afshan ask, darling, why did you stopped yourself? Please tell me, what do you mean by “but”? Fazal comments, I’m a bit apprehensive about this Indian folks, Afshan reacts, surprisingly, wonders, and queries, sweetheart, why do you have to be apprehensive about Indians? They will pay you money and your job is to work for the sake of money.

Afshan shrugs off, Fazal’s fear, she says, don’t you worry, there’s nothing wrong that’s going to happen, hoping the deal that this Indian journalist is offering will be lucrative opportunity, please go ahead and meet him on optimistic note, allay all your concern.

Fazal agrees, commits to Afshan, yes, ok, fix my appointment with the visiting Indian journalist “Sudhir Singh,” Afshan gets up from her chair and gives a warm hug to Fazal and says, that’s like a “true Afghan Pashtun Geezer” I liked this aggressive approach of yours, Fazal kisses Afshan and thanks her for the compliments.

Afshan khan reminds Fazal, sweetheart, please don’t forget to give me my share of money once your deal is struck with the Indian journalist, Fazal replies, oh, sure babes, how can I ever forget to give you your share of money, but for time being you fix my appointment with “Sudhir Singh,” Afshan commits, ok, dear, I’ll immediately go to meet “Sudhir Singh” who apparently must be eagerly waiting to get response from me, so I’ll meet him and fix the exact time and location of the meeting and inform you, Fazal nods his head, ok, that will be fine with me, please let me know.

Afshan scrapes her hair arranges her fringe, adjust her clothes looks into the mirror to see if she’s looking appropriate than picks up her hand bag, Afshan passionately kisses Fazal and tells him, how much she enjoyed her vices with him, Fazal replies, I’m humbled to have enjoyed virtue and vices to with hot and sexy woman like you, Afshan cravingly response, love you are an amazing man, no matter how much time I spend with you there’s always a urge to spend even more time with you, Afshan adds, how privilege are those two women who have got the honour of becoming your wife, Afshan ask, sweet heart are you feeling the urge for additional woman in your life, is there an opportunity left for me to become your third “better half,” Fazal spanks Afshan says, you naughty woman “No” two wives are enough for me, I’ve no desire and there’s no need for me to marry a third woman, Afshan keeping up with her floozy reputation says, you, how rude a man you are, you ferociously contorted me, played with me all night, but you can't make me your third wife, Fazal vociferates, you naughty woman please go and fix appointment with that Indian friend of yours.

Afshan jokingly says, why do you tell me "naughty woman"? How rude you creep, why don't you say "naughty girl"? am I so old to not to be called a "girl," Fazal fumes and stares at Afshan, and Afshan says, ok, my love, bye, now I'm going and sorry but, I love to bother you and make you angry that's why I was kidding and fooling with you, Fazal cling Afshan kisses her, Afshan finally concludes meeting with Fazal and departs from his hotel suite.

Afshan approaches the visiting Indian journalist "Sudhir Singh" conveys to him that Fazal khan Bangash has agreed to meet him and has shown interest in working for him, Sudhir Singh gives his consent, Afshan fixes time and venue for the clandestine meeting between Indian journalist "Sudhir and Fazal" at mutually agreed location.

Chapter 17

The dusk has fallen and late evening ever so confident Fazal Khan Bangash swaggers his way out of the hotel gets in to a private car and he drives the car himself, Fazal drives the car on outskirt of Lahore city at an undisclosed location to meet Indian journalist Sudhir Singh, Fazal reaches the destination which is a small resort hotel where the room is booked and Sudhir Singh has already arrived and is waiting for Fazal to enter the room to hold one to one close door meeting.

Fazal enters the room, both Indian journalist "Sudhir Singh" and Fazal warmly greets each other, there's no one present in the room, as this meeting is highly secretive.

Fazal and Sudhir starts meeting by first exchanging pleasantries and begin with small talks which are trivia in nature.

Sudhir ask Fazal, shall we now talk business, Fazal nods, Yes, let's talk business, Sudhir Singh starts conversation, he comments jokingly, it's not business but its politics, Fazal responses, in terror world politics or business both are same side of same coin for us.

Sudhir says, I liked what you just said, I'm seeing in your eyes which is dazzling with confidence and am sure to strike a deal with you, Fazal as well talks fire with fire, he assertively replies, that's an incredible skills you have, of peeping into the eyes of your opponent and to understand the motives as well as objectives of your opponents, as it is the true attributes and the real motives of any person is not in how he/she talks and his/her body language behaves, but the real truth of the person lies in his eyes, because we can only listen and see the person body language, we have no access to the thoughts of a person, Fazal tells to Sudhir, you seem to be a good negotiator, it will be nice to strike intimate deal with you.

Sudhir comments, the deal is to cause immense damage and destruction to public lives and their properties," Fazal painstakingly listens to Sudhir Singh, Sudhir ask Fazal, do you by any chance follow Indian politics? Fazal comments, economics and politics runs in my blood, I exquisitely keep track of economic and political developments happening around the world.

Sudhir acknowledges Fazal and ask him, so you must be knowing that in four months from now India is heading for its compulsory midterm general election, Fazal nods, yes, I know it well.

Sudhir Singh says, look as both of us common friend "Afshan Khan" must have informed you about me, she must have told you that I'm a journalist and work for private TV News channel as News Anchor, Fazal responses, yes, she has very well briefed me about you and the profession you are in.

Sudhir says, excellent, than, he further adds, we journalist have to deal with this politicians also the folks from corporate and glamour world on day to day basis, Sudhir Singh explains, to be honest with you we journalist officially earn very little money, Fazal nods head, ok, what more, Sudhir add, most of them from the profession of journalism don't even get paid their monthly salary on time, Fazal empathize, oh, that's a very disturbing fact, so, how does folks from media makes there ends meet?

Sudhir grins, than answers, we have to find source of supplement income, and the inside information is, Fazal curiously, ask, what? Sudhir comments, most people from journalist for survival becomes frontman or liaise (wheeler and dealer) and secretly works for corrupt government officials and the politicians and many others like wicked businessman also for "Don's" from underworld and many others, Sudhir elaborates, many of us "the journalist" help people with dubious and outrageously corrupt people from society in many ways, by acting as there agent helping them strike nefarious deals and negotiate on their behalf with their opponents and their peers.

Fazal nods his head, yes, friend, I've understood exactly what you mean to says, Fazal comments, this is the "NARCISSISTIC SOCIETY," every people have single point agenda and sole motive which is gain "power and wealth."

Sudhir agrees with Fazal, yes, you're right, we are all "Narcissistic," Fazal sarcastically laughs, hah, hah, hah, says, you forgot to mention one critical game many in particularly from your journalist fraternity plays, Sudhir queries, what? Fazal says, "Blackmail" these fellows carry out sting operation or they access some incriminating documents and then they resort to blackmailing either the politicians, businessman or professionals, Sudhir Singh reacts with sheepish smile and acknowledges the unsubstantiated fact.

Sudhir Singh says, ok, let me now discuss with you the real topic, for which this meeting between you and me have been arranged, Fazal says, yes, please start the real discussion.

Sudhir begins, he ask Fazal, as you keep yourself update with national and international politics, Fazal make hum sound, Sudhir ask, you must have heard the name of one of the top politician in contemporary Indian politics that of "Mr Hiren Todi," Fazal confirms, yes, this man "Mr Todi" is currently serving Chief Minister of one of the Indian province and also he's aspiring to become next Prime Minister of India, am I correct, Sudhir replies, 100% correct.

Sudhir adds, Now the point is, that today I'm meeting you at his behest, I'm striking the deal with you, in the capacity of an agent and I have been given the responsibility to negotiate with you on behalf on Mr Todi and the political party "The' Bharat Party" that he represents, Sudhir explains, This political party the "Bharat Party" is presently the principle opposition party in India, and now Bharat Party is making desperate attempt to seized power in India, Bharat Party wants to become the ruling party of India.

Fazal painstakingly listens to Sudhir, Sudhir says, as you may be knowing that in next four months general election are to be held in India, and India is a very large and diverse country, India's population consist of many different religion and religious minorities and various different ethnic groups and hundreds of different language are spoken across the country, there are also linguistic minorities.

Fazal acknowledges, yes I'm aware of Indian culture and its demographics, Sudhir continues, in India to win election for the political parties is no simple task, because of so many different regions and religions and linguistic minorities, there are persistent demands and discontent among the masses, the people are never satisfied with the politicians as because this politicians can never fulfil their obligation towards there electorates and never can the ever keep their commitments nor are they ever interested in fulfilling their promises because the politicians for the five year terms that they are elected, they keep themselves busy filling their pockets with money.

Fazal ask, what is it that I can do for you? What role do you want me to play? Sudhir replies, as I'm representing the top politician of India "Mr Hiren Todi" and Mr Todi has position himself to become the Prime Minister of India and his Political party is considered to be a Right Wing Hindu Nationalist Party, The Political ideology and the attributes of Bharat Party is more or less similar to, for, Eg; The Neo Nazi's of Europe or the "Salafist" Islamic Extremist.

Sudhir add, the purpose behind this nefarious act of "Blasting Sites" are obvious, the objective is to cause flutter in civil society and this political party "Bharat Party" will use this blasts as catalyst to radicalize and polarise people belonging majority and minorities communities, and thereby score political capital and consolidate its position and this what will help the "Bharat party" win national election.

Sudhir tells Fazal, we want you to make arrangement to carry out "Blast," Fazal ask, how many blast and of what intensity? Low intensity blast or major blast.

Sudhir says, you'll have to arrange for Two Large Intensity Blast, in Two major urban Indian cities, Fazal ask, do you want us to carry out huge Bomb Explosion? Shall I arrange for big "RDX Material Bomb Explosions," Sudhir nods his head, yes, exactly use the harmful substance "The RDX" and blast 'Two" major urban cities, Fazal queries, any particular city or cities? Sudhir answers, from two cities, One city in western India and other Town in Central

India, Sudhir add, you will have to organize Blasting these Two cities any day in next Twenty Days.

Sudhir further says, ensure the blast happens on the weekdays and it should be blasted in a crowded place, also ensure the explosive material have some kind of Islamic literature printed or written on it so that when the investigation is held, the needle of suspicion should point towards the Islamic jihadist, This is the most crucial part of the whole drama, because this Political party which planning this attack is as I said Right wing Hindu Party, and the blame of the blast on the Islamic jihadist will suit its purpose because after all this bloodbath is being orchestrated for the purpose to ignite the passion and communal feeling among the majority Indian population which "Hindu."

Fazal reconfirms, so this Indian Political party is orchestrating this Twin Bomb Blast to radicalize a large section of Indian population and thereby polarize the vote bank, this is the objective of "Bharat Party" and its top leader there appointed "Prime Ministerial" candidate Mr Hiren Todi.

Fazal add, the best I know of this gentleman "Mr Hiren Todi" is that he's a compulsive betrayer and arguably the most wicked and monstrous man, Mr Todi has a reputation of betraying, he betrayed his father when he was a young boy, than he married a young girl and cheated on her, he deceit her ran away and later in recent past he has deceit all the senior member of his own political party "The' Bharat Party," Sudhir Singh laughs hysterically and acknowledges what Fazal said about the ever so wicked Indian politician Mr Todi.

Fazal assures Sudhir, tells him, your work will be done, and rest assure there won't be any error from our side, Fazal comments, I have a team of extremely well trained Mujahideen and Fedayeen (the men ready to fight and sacrifice their life for the sake of religion), Sudhir says, that will be fine, Sudhir also says, the two bomb blast needs to be in sync, the blast in two separate town and city, yet it should be coordinated in such a way the blast occurs at the same time, the blast needs to be so powerful that it should devastate the whole country.

Fazal assures him, not to worry the blast will have catastrophic impact on the social and civil lives and the minds of not only Indians but the international community will also feel the jitters.

Fazal stares into the eyes of the negotiator "the Indian journalist' Sudhir Singh," than ask, him, my friend you've discussed everything with me accept, Sudhir understand what Fazal is asking him.

Sudhir says, we'll pay you an engaging amount for doing this job of blasting, Fazal ask, how much' buddy? Sudhir Singh discloses the offer price, you'll get astronomical sum of money "Ten Million US Dollars" cash.

Fazal agrees, confirm, it's a deal, Fazal shakes hand with Sudhir Singh and assures him again, your job will be done, immaculately.

Sudhir Singh happy to seal the deal of blasting two Indian cities with Fazal khan Bangash.

Fazal while conversing with Sudhir asks him, I want to know your opinion, are the people of India so naïve that they will trust this conman "Mr Todi" and in sympathy vote for him in the forthcoming election, Sudhir emphatically replies, yes, don't you know the same Bharat Party had earlier fooled the public of India in the name of Hindu gods, they had earlier as well successfully cheated and deceit the majority Indian population and once the blast happens before elections, this same Indian public, or to say a large chunk of the majority Hindu population will show remorse and will have illusion that only this "Bharat Party" can save them from Islamic extremist terrorist and these fools will once again vote for the communal 'Bharat Party.

Fazal says, ok, what the hell? Why should I be concern, I simply do the job for the sake of money, as you are giving us money, I'll do the job for you, Fazal adds, but what an irony is it the Hindu fundamental are using Islamic militancy to kill their own people.

Sudhir Singh says, this is how the life goes, because this lot of people always remains intellectually duffer, Fazal says, it's because of this intellectually bankruptcy people, the cunning and shrewd people like us thrive, Sudhir Singh comprehends Fazal's view, he says, I couldn't agree with you more than what you just said, in fool's paradise the smartest thrives.

The meeting between Fazal Khan Bangash and Sudhir Singh concludes on happy note, both of them depart form the secret location a resort where the two of them held meeting.

Fazal returns back to his luxurious hotel suite, late in the night past midnight feeling overwhelmingly fatigue after intense discussion with Sudhir Singh, Fazal after a couple of tots of whiskey and some light food recline on bed and doze off to sleep.

The dawn breaks out, Fazal wakes up, on his part the Indian journalist and the chief negotiator Sudhir Singh through his agent delivers an advance instalment of "Two Million US Dollars" to Fazal's agent.

After confined largely in his hotel room for a day, it's time now for Fazal to act, Fazal takes a flight to Yemeni City of Sanaa, from Yemen, Fazal boards into a speedboat and crosses the sea and enters the Somalian territory, and he drives inside the perilous Somalian countryside and reaches the bushy jungles of Somalia, to the "Al Noora jihadist camp" Fazal meets his friend and mentor the Al Noora jihadist organization chief "Waqar Iqbal."

Waqar warmly welcomes Fazal, greets him, both Fazal and Waqar have met after long time so both have lots to discuss, after conversing for few minutes, Fazal tells Waqar, my friend, I have come to meet you today for a purpose, there is a deal that I've struck with an agent of a principle opposition political party of India "The' Bharat Party" and its top leader "Mr Hiren Todi."

Waqar visibly happy, tell me, my friend, my brother, what is the deal? I'll be more than happy to work for you, Fazal replies, yes the deal is final and now I have to execute the deal and for which I need your help.

Waqar listens, ask, what deal? I'm willing to help you, Fazal explains, the deal is to devastate two urban Indian cities, one city in western India and other town in central India.

Waqar nods his head, yes, it's possible for us, tell me more, Fazal add, you have to arrange the jihadist to detonate two high intensity "Bomb Blast" RDX material should be used to have catastrophic impact.

Fazal elaborates, this blast needs to be in sync and both the blast needs to be executed at the same time.

Waqar assures Fazal, yes, the work will be done as you want us to, Fazal replies, excellent, the offer to you is "Five Million US Dollars," Waqar listens the offer price which Fazal has quoted him, Waqar frowns and takes deep breath, Waqar confirms, ok, tell me, when do I have to arrange the blast in the two Indian cities?

Fazal replies, any day in the next fifteen days, but, the blast should be executed on a weekday, and the time should be in the evening between 5pm to 7.30pm in a crowded locality of the city.

Waqar tells Fazal, tomorrow itself I'll plan the attack and day after tomorrow I'll depute two of my most trusted jihadist militant on the assignment, they will embark on the journey to India within two days from now, Fazal says to Waqar, "brother" I trust y'all and have complete faith in your skills to carry out snuck attacks, but, still, please ensure, that there is no error, Waqar comments, my friend, it will be immaculately planned attack, no room for any error.

Fazal after spending one whole day in the "Al Noora jihadist camp" gets ready to start his journey back home to "Kabul" before living from the camp, Fazal tells Waqar, my agent will deliver the promised amount of money (Five Million US Dollar) to your agent in next 48 hours, Waqar nods his head, yes, that will be good for us, Fazal set himself to move out of AL Noora jihadist camp, Waqar gives a genial send off to Fazal.

Waqar Iqbal the chief of the jihadist group "Al Noora" starts getting his act together, Waqar summons two of his trusted lieutenant "Razzak and Salim," Waqar perspicuously briefs both "Razzak and Salim" that they have to embark on journey to India to carry out snuck attack on two separate "key Indian urban cities," each located in western and central part of India.

Waqar add, informs his two men "Razzak and Salim" that each of them have to take responsibility of each city, Waqar further explains his men, they'll have to contact members of their Al Noora jihadist group's Indian associate jihadist group of "Al Mujahideen" and take its help, Waqar tells both "Razzak and Salim" to take help of few members from the sleeping cell of "Al Mujahideen's," because those jihadist are the local Indians hence they'll have better understanding in regards to exact places where the "RDX Bombs" have to be exploded, and then plan the attack on the Indian cities.

Razzak and Salim, in one voice assures there boss “Waqar” that they’ve understood the plan and they are mentally fully prepared to strike at Indian targets, Waqar assertively comments, please ensure, the “Bomb Blast” should be of massive intensity and that it resonate and reverberate across the globe.

Razzak and Salim assures there boss “Waqar” indeed, have faith in us, the blast in the Indian town will resonate the world over, Waqar hugs both “Razzak and Salim” and wishes them “Good luck.”

Razzak and Salim overwhelmingly confident and embolden after seeking blessing from there chief “Waqar” and other senior members of Al Noora jihadist group, both Razzak and Salim on optimistic note leaves the Al Noora jihadist camp in Somalia and embarks on the journey to India on the perilous mission of exploding RDX Bomb in the two Indian cities.

Razzak and Salim first destination on their way to India is Pakistani port city of Karachi, where they meet there associate member “Rafiq Raja,” Rafiq provides Razzak and Salim explosive materials “RDX” and he also helps Razzak and Salim cross over inside the Indian territory, through Pakistani border.

Razzak and Salim base themselves in a small town not very far away from Indo-Pak border, Salim establishes contact with the Indian chief of “Al Mujahideen jihadist group,” he request the chief of “Al Mujahideen” to provide them the service of at least four jihadist members from the “Al Mujahideen” sleeping cell, the chief of Indian “Al Mujahideen” commits his full cooperation to Salim.

Salim and Razzak than separately embarks on a two day journey of the Indian cities which they are contemplating blasting, while Razzak takes charge of blasting the central Indian town, hence Salim has to take responsibility of blasting the western Indian city, both Razzak and Salim goes separately on the recce of Indian city.

Salim and Razzak finish there recce of the city they want to blast, in mean time the four members from the Indian “Al Mujahideen” as well assemble where Razzak and Salim are staying, Razzak takes over the responsibility of dividing work, Razzak tells the four jihadist members from the sleeping cell of “Al Mujahideen” that, they’ll be divided into two groups, two members should accompany Salim and other two members should accompany him to central Indian city, Razzak also hands the material “RDX Bomb” to the jihadist members of Indian "Al Mujahideen" and briefs them, as in, how to explode the Bomb in the crowded market, the four members from the sleeping cell of Indian "Al Mujahideen" conveys there resolve to fight against the infidels and assures that they would mercilessly blast the Indian city and take revenge of the blood of their community members.

Razzak applauds there intent, says, yes, our religion is in danger, the infidels are aggressively harming interest of our community hence we should show or have no remorse for these damn infidels, each of the members present vociferates, yes, kill the infidels.

Chapter 18

The day is Wednesday, its late evening, Razzak along with two Indian associate has taken position in the central Indian town and at other end his colleague Salim and other two Indian associates have taken position in the western Indian city.

The time is 6.05 pm, the dusk is above to fall, the busy shopping area is bustling, lots of crowd on the street are busy shopping and many of them have flock around the eatery joints, enjoying hot Indian snacks, Razzak makes a phone call to his colleague Salim, the two colleagues mumbo jumbo, Razzak inquires with Salim, ask him, are you ready? Salim replies, yes, we are ready to go, Razzak says, in next precisely "Five Minutes" the noise should be heard (referring to Bomb explosion), Salim nods, ok, done, the noise will resonate all over, Razzak says, over and out.

Salim informs the two members of the Indian "Al Mujahideen" set yourself, go ahead and Blast the "Bomb' RDX" the two members nods there head, and moves forward to plant the Bomb.

Razzak does the same instructs the two Indian jihadist members to go ahead and blast the "RDX' Bomb," Razzak moves backwards and prepares himself to run away from the site.

Salim moves backwards and vamoose, Razzak moves back and vamoose from the potential blast site.

The jihadist members from the sleeping cell of Indian "Al Mujahideen Fedayeen group" all set to explode the "RDX Bomb."

The time is set and The Bomb explodes, Two Prominent Urban Indian Cities are rocked with powerful bomb explosion, loud noise reverberates, shops and buildings in the area are decimated by powerful explosion, many people's bodies are torn apart beyond recognition, total chaos has broken out, many buildings are on fire, huge flames can be seen from long distance.

Razzak and Salim are on the run, at least two out of four members of the Indian jihadist "Al Mujahideen" also killed remaining two are on run, but, wait, No, one of the jihadist from sleeping cell of India jihadist group "Al Mujahideen" is nabbed by police while he was trying to escape from the city, as he was moving rather suspiciously, the jihadist caught his name is "Amjad."

There is panic stricken all over India, emotions are running high among Indians, the political circle is jittery, wide spread condemnation pours from across the world, all the prominent news channels all over the world are covering this harrowing incident, hundreds of innocent people have lost their life, many parents have lost their children, many children's have become orphan.

The politicians are trading barbs, the principle opposition party "The Bharat Party" also considered to be right wing Hindu party is bitterly condemning the ruling party accusing it to be soft stance towards the minorities.

The politicians will shamelessly play politics over the "Dead Bodies" they will as ever trade barbs, but it's the common men from the street who suffers.

Here again the principle conspirator and the key mastermind behind these two high intensity bomb blast, "Mr Hiren Todi" is cheerful he's gaining popularity by shedding crocodile tears.

Both, Mr Hiren Todi and his party "The Bharat Party" are euphoric as now with national general elections in India are just three months away and by politicising the dastardly committed inhuman heinous crime, they intend making political gain out of it.

Razzak and Salim manages to sneak out of the Indian Territory, on the other side into Pakistani Territory and through Pakistan's border they manages to reach back to their base in the bushy jungles of Somalia.

Fazal khan Bangash gets his share of money from the agent of the Indian Power broker and agent of top Indian politician “Mr Hiren Todi.”

Fazal is enjoying every moment of his life, Fazal’s second wife “Hala” is heavily pregnant, so now the onus is on his first wife “Yalda” to take care of him.

Fazal enjoys babysitting for his daughter “Nagma” he also has the twin responsibility of his other half sibling and now also his stepdaughter “Heena” Fazal adores Heena a lot and plays with her.

Yalda a submissive wife ensures her husband is well entertained, as her co-wife “Hala” is out of action due to her pregnancy, hence Yalda has to work overtime during the day time in kitchen and at night in the bedroom, devoutly, performing her marital obligation by passionately indulging with her husband.

Fazal enjoying his leisure time with his two wives and kids, and happily waiting to welcome his own second child from his second wife “Hala.”

Fazal receives a phone call from the same Pakistani woman, the socialite and TV journalist “Miss Afshan Khan.”

Afshan only makes a brief telephonic conversation with Fazal, Afshan tells him, there is a potential deal, if interested please visit my hometown Lahore and meet me, Fazal gives his nods, tells Afshan, ok, I’ll come to meet you tomorrow.

Fazal summons both his wives “Yalda and Hala” and tells them that tomorrow morning, I have to embark on my supposedly business trip, Yalda resents, oh, dear, but, why? You live us alone and go on long business trips of yours, Fazal apologizes and convince her, my wife, it’s a question of bread and butter, it’s part of my business to keep travelling, his second wife who’s herself a former jihadist “Hala” hugs her co-wife “Yalda” and convince her, let him go he’s doing whatever he’s doing for betterment of our family.

Yalda comments, when you go on your business trip, I feel premonitory, Fazal shrugs off her talk and allays her fear, he tells Yalda, you are wife of an incredibly brave man, please don’t worry, Yalda hugs Fazal, says, my best wishes with you my dear husband, please go happily on your business excursion.

Next morning, Fazal lives behind his wives at home and steps out of his house and commences his journey to Pakistan, Fazal flies to Pakistani city of Lahore.

Fazal's flight lands at Lahore airport, Fazal checks-in to the hotel, after settling down in his hotel room and after taking some refreshment, it's time for Fazal to start working.

Fazal contacts the Pakistani journalist Miss Afshan khan, Fazal speaks to Afshan over the phone, Afshan request Fazal to come and meet her at a secret location in downtown Lahore city.

Late afternoon Fazal steps out of his hotel room and goes to meet the intriguing lady the stunning socialite and journalist "Miss Afshan Khan."

At an undisclosed location in the most remote part of Lahore city donning Black Burqa (black veil) Afshan arrives to meet Fazal.

Fazal greets Afshan with loud "As-Salamu-Alay-Kum" she replies back "WalayKum-As-Salam," Afshan lifts the veil from her face and tells Fazal, we have to quickly wrap our meeting, Afshan add, I fear there could be someone from intelligence following us, even though this is just my assumption, but, we've to be careful.

Fazal comprehends, ok, I understand, tell me, why have you call me to meet you? What's the deal? Afshan comments, there's a terror deal, a mysterious party obviously with ulterior motives wants to strike a deal again the deal as always would be potentially destructive in nature.

Fazal ask, who's that mysterious party? Afshan replies, No, I have absolutely no clue, as in, who those people are, Fazal retorts, than, how will we work for them? Afshan inquires, first you tell me, are you game? Are you willing to strike a deal with that mysterious party? Fazal nods his head, yes.

Afshan add, that's good, I knew you'll never say, No, Afshan elaborates, if you are willing you'll have to travel all the way to "Oman" once you reach Oman, a gentleman whose name is "Yarden," this gentleman Yarden will personally contact you in the hotel where you would be staying and from there he will personally guide you and take you along with him to meet a young lady, Afshan add, now, who this young lady is? Please, don't ask me, as even I'm unaware of who this lady is.

Afshan elucidates, this potentially destructive deal is being planned in a highly secretive and a very "hush, hush" manner, Afshan add, there is tremendous immanent risk involve in this deal.

Fazal after painstakingly listening to Afshan replies, don't worry, I've learnt to play with fire, I like playing fire with fire.

Afshan smirks, she never misses opportunity to make lewd comments, in reply to Fazal rhetoric, she comments, darling you just now talked about playing fire with fire, Fazal makes hum sound, Afshan says, darling you can't understand my feeling what a woman wants from the man she so overwhelmingly like, whenever I see you, my body starts to shudder, the flames that emanates from the fire in you makes me perspire my body gets wet, oh, gosh, my body smells, Afshan stops from talking further and says, oh, gosh, I just couldn't control my emotion, I forgot this is very sensitive meeting between us.

Fazal comments, you naughty woman, you are always up to your vices, Afshan says, we will play our vices once your deal is over but for now let us conclude our meeting the dusk is above to fall, and we both better go back before anyone spots us, Fazal says, ok, Afshan gaze into Fazal's eyes, says, please be careful and good luck to you, negotiate the deal well.

Fazal and Afshan concludes there clandestine meeting and go the separate ways to their respective bases.

Fazal returns back to his hotel room, Fazal recumbent on bed racks up his brain, he wonders who must be those mysterious people or group, for, whom I may have to work? Fazal vividly thinks and mentally prepares himself for negotiation with the discreet "party."

With mounting unease, but on highly optimistic note, Fazal takes a flight to Oman and reaches Oman for the clandestine meeting.

Fazal checks-in the upscale Five Star Hotel, Fazal spends a night in the five star hotel room, next morning first thing he does is to take plunge in the swimming pool, Fazal spends over an hour swimming in a swanky swimming pool, than he walks into a nearly deserted restaurant of the hotel to eat breakfast.

Fazal is waiting for a local Arab gentleman "Yarden" to contact him, Fazal bit impatient, its afternoon and the Arab gentleman is still not appearing, Fazal calls hotel room service and orders lunch for himself.

Finally late afternoon Fazal receives a call, a gentleman says to him, he's come to meet him and that he's speaking to him from downstairs from the hotel lobby, he ask Fazal, may I walk up to your room and meet you in person.

Fazal breathes easy, he replies, yes, please come, you're most welcome.

The man walks upstairs knock on Fazal's door and Fazal opens the door and welcomes him inside the room, the gentleman introduces himself as "Yarden," he ask Fazal, Miss Afshan Khan may have briefed you about me, Fazal nods his head, yes.

Yarden ask, shall we move than, are you ready to accompany me to meet a "Lady" who's waiting to meet you, Fazal replies, yes, give me ten minutes to get ready, Yarden replies, sure, take your time, I'm waiting for you downstairs in the lobby, Fazal replies, ok, that will be fine, wait for me in the lobby downstairs, and I'll be downstairs in few minutes, Yarden says, ok, and steps out of the room.

Fazal dresses up, donning formal suit and wearing designer sunglasses looking no less than a Hollywood film "Hero," Fazal steps out of his hotel room, swaggers down to the hotel lobby, he approaches Yarden and the two get into the Car, Yarden drives the Car to the luxurious beach resort.

Fazal and Yarden reaches the resort, where a lady agent of the "mysterious organization" is staying.

Yarden request Fazal to wait for few moments in the resorts reception area, while he first go and meet the intriguing lady to inform her about your arrival, Fazal says, ok, I'll wait for you.

Yarden first speak to the lady on the hotel intercom, than he walks up to the room that is occupied by the "lady' agent," Yarden meets the lady and she gives her consent and ask Yarden to send Fazal Khan Bangash inside her room to hold close door meeting with her.

Yarden tells the lady "Agent" as you wish, Yarden comes to the lobby and request Fazal to accompany him and walk up to the room of the "lady Agent."

Fazal walks inside the room, Yarden introduces Fazal to "the agent of mysterious organization," she's an amazing beauty, Yarden introduce her to Fazal and tells Fazal meet her she's "Jessica."

Jessica graciously greets Fazal with a warm handshake, Jessica is an elegant blonde woman, Yarden after introducing Jessica to Fazal, than he walks out of the room.

Fazal and Jessica starts conversation with exchanging pleasantries, after small talk, Jessica tells Fazal, I won't disclose to you any information as in, who I'm? or, what is the name of the organization? Which apparently is interested in hiring you and assign you to carry out destructive snuck attack etc.

Jessica add, to be candid with you, quite an irony, the fact is that even though I'm hired to brief you and negotiate with you a destructive deal, even I'm personally oblivious of the fact, as in, who are the real people? Where are they from? Obviously theirs is a sly motive, everything part of this terror deal is being conducted in highly secretive way, but, what are their objectives behind striking terror attack at sensitive targets, it's anyone's guess, and better we don't bother ourselves dwelling over it, rather we do our job and get paid for doing our "Narcissistic" duty.

Fazal listens to Jessica's comments, than, replies, well I bother the least as in who this mysterious people or organizations are or is, I work for money, and striking terror has become an adventure for me.

Fazal add, now, you tell me, what is the deal? What do you expect from me? How may I help you? Jessica tells, terrorise the world is what you'll have to do.

Fazal nods, ok, please, perspicuously explain to me, when and where do y'all want me to organize attack? What are the potential targets that has to be blasted?

Jessica says, as the nature of deal is aggressive and destructive, also before I come to the point and disclose to you exact nature of the work, let me also categorically let you know, that, this is potentially most imperilled assignment, that you may have ever dealt with.

Fazal stares deep into the green dazzling eyes of Jessica than delivers dialogue, says, "passive aggression send wrong signals and my aggression is pragmatic," for me, the bigger the risk the more satisfying is the fulfilment of working on a deal.

Jessica replies, that's precisely the reason, why we've approach you to take charge of the deal, Jessica add, before approaching you, we've had learnt from our reliable sources about your proficiency and courage.

Jessica says, ok, now, let me tell you, precisely what we want you to do, Fazal responses, yes, please, tell me.

Jessica elaborates, there are two responsibility you need to take, the first is that you will have to organize a "fanatic" fundamentalist jihadist man.

Jessica add, these "fanatic jihadist man" will have to attack people on the street of Paris.

Fazal ask, what exactly he has to do, Jessica explains, this fanatic jihadist will have to run amok on moderately busy street of French city of "Paris," he will have to hold a big sharp pointed knife in his hand and he will have start shouting religious slogans and recite religious sermons and he will have to randomly attack few people, these fanatic jihadist will have to randomly and brutally stab and severely injure as many pedestrian as he could on the street with the big sharp pointed knife.

Fazal ask, what happens afterwards, Jessica comments, after he completes attacking and brutally injuring pedestrians, he should try to escape from the site, though he'll apparently be caught but he should try to resist being arrested, may be, what happens is that he may get killed in the police encounter, or if he wish to he can commit suicide, Jessica tells Fazal, basically whatever happen just live that fanatic jihadist to his fate, our objective will be achieved once he brutally attacks few pedestrians on the street of Paris.

Fazal nods his head, ok, what next? Jessica replies, the next thing is the most perilous mission, ever to be carried out, Fazal questions, what is it? Jessica comments, the next thing you have to arrange for is to attack ships in the waters of Persian sea.

Fazal frowns, oh, that's a very nasty one, Jessica comprehends, yes, this is the most difficult of the terror strike, but, this job has to be done.

Fazal says, ok, please elaborate, Jessica says, you have to arrange an attack in the middle of the Persian sea, and you have to carry out snuck attack on any two of the large vessel, Jessica add, what I mean is, your jihadist militants can randomly select any two large ships that would be sailing is the Persian sea, and attack those ships, also ensure the ships that should be attacked and decimated should be the cargo ship loaded with delivery of crude oil in it.

Jessica adds, the attack should be of very high intensity, and once the two ships those are attacked, the ships should get obliterate, Jessica says, both the ship will have to be attacked and blasted in short span of time.

Fazal comments, the assignment you want to render me is extremely dangerous, but, I like to accept difficult challenges, Fazal assures Jessica, your job will be done.

Jessica reacts, wow, that's fantastic, I like the confident with which you said, that you like to play with fire, you like accepting difficult challenges, Fazal smirks, yes, I'm not a safety player, when I'm most active I enunciate every possible choice and options I have at my command to achieve my objectives.

Jessica says, excellent, she cautions Fazal, says, as we are planning this heinous crime of attacking sensitive world targets to cause flutter in the global civil society.

Jessica add, at the same time there are several government agency who all have got whiff of the evil motive of this mysterious organization for whom you and I are planning attack, hence these several federal governments agencies are at work, they are secretly and covertly working towards ensuring safety of the potential targets which are on the terror hit list and thereby readying themselves with apparatus to thwart our nefarious plan.

Fazal replies, don't worry, I survive under the seedy and belly of underworld, hence, I've learnt to stay a step ahead of law.

Jessica compliments Fazal for his courage and confidence.

Fazal ask, ok, now, the big question, how much will y'all pay me?

Jessica replies, we are ready to pay you unprecedented amount of money, Fazal queries, how much? Jessica offers, we pay you "Thirty Million US Dollars," Jessica after disclosing offer amount to Fazal, she stares at him.

Fazal pause for a while, nods his head, ok, sounds good, I accept your offer of "Thirty Million US Dollars," Jessica ask, so, is it final, should I tell my bosses that I've successfully struck a deal of striking the "terror attack" with you.

Fazal confirms, yes, The Deal is Seal" between we all mysterious persons.

Jessica gets up from the chair she's sitting on from across the table and extends her hand, for handshake, Fazal warmly shakes hands with the negotiator "Jessica."

The marathon one on one meeting session between Jessica and Fazal is over, Fazal walks into the lobby of the beach resort, Yarden has had to wait for long time spending time chatting with few people and reading boring newspapers, Fazal apologises to Yarden, sorry, friend, you had a long wait for me, Yarden gracious enough, replies, with beaming smile, absolutely no problem, friend. Fazal gets inside Yarden's car and comes back to his hotel where he is staying.

Overwhelmingly tired, Fazal takes few tots of brandy, than calls hotel room service orders food for dinner, Fazal spends most of the night awake, outrageously worried as in how I will coordinate and executes my ideas of striking terror.

Chapter 19

With mounting horror, Fazal embarks on his second leg of the journey to Somalia, Fazal boards an aircraft and flies to the Kenyan city of "Nairobi," and from Nairobi he drives all the way through the most treacherous terrain across the border and enters the Somalian territory, Fazal reaches the "Al Noora jihadist camp," Fazal than holds one on one discussion session with chief of Al Noora jihadist group "Waqar Iqbal."

Fazal briefs Waqar about the nature of the intimate deal he has struck with a mysterious organization.

Fazal tells Waqar, the deal I've struck with a lady negotiator of the mysterious organization is, Waqar ask, what? Fazal elucidates, there two parts to the deal, "first" is, that a religious jihadist man should run amok on the street of French city of "Paris," holding a big knife in his hand and he should randomly attack pedestrians and brutally stab and wound nearly a dozen or so pedestrian on the street and ensure the ones he stabs with knife are severely wounded, even if some of the pedestrian injured by default "dies" that's not a problem, the purpose behind this attack is to cause flutter in the civic society.

Fazal add, the man who carries out this snuck attack in Paris should be a religious fanatic, he should recite religious sermons while attacking the pedestrian, once he's done with attacking people he either run away from the scene or just live himself to the fate, either he'll be killed in police encounter or he kills himself or he may get arrested.

Waqar nods his head, ok, I have understood, what your first part of the deal is? Now tell me, what's the second part of the deal?

Fazal smirks than replies, the second part of the deal is most horrendous, Waqar smirks, ask, it seems perilous, but let me listen, Fazal comments, the second part of the deal and what you apparently have to do is to attack a "tanker" a ship loaded with crude oil which is on its journey to whichever destination, while the ship is sailing in the waters of Persian Sea, that's when these ships have to be attacked, Fazal elaborates, not one but you have to randomly select any two such ships which are loaded with crude oil and sailing in the waters of Persian Sea and are on its way to its destination, have to blasted right in the middle of the sea, the blast should be of a very high intensity, the ships must get decimated.

Waqar after painstakingly listening to Fazal, comments, both the incidents will be planned and put into effect, Waqar add, blasting the ship is difficult but not impossible, we have associates who are otherwise "Pirates" and they have the expertise of carrying out such attacks, such as attacking the ships right in the middle of the water, Waqar elaborates, many of our jihadist may also loss their lives while attacking the ships in the Persian Sea.

Fazal acknowledges, yes, there is an immanent risk, many of your men's may also loss their lives.

Waqar agrees, ok, don't worry it's our job to play with fire and carry out dangerous attacks, not a problem, Waqar ask, tell me, how much money are you ready to pay us?

Fazal says, I'll pay y'all astronomical sum of money, Waqar response, ok. That's very good, let me hear it from you, Fazal offers, "Fifteen Million US Dollars."

Waqar enraptures, wow, that's a very enticing a very fetching amount, I agree to your deal, lets seal it now, Fazal responses, excellent, lets shake hands than.

Waqar says, I seldom move out of this intimate Somali jihadist camp of mine, but to execute your deal, I'll have to personally move out of this camp, first I'll have to slyly go to French city of "Paris" because we have members of our jihadist groups "Al Noora" spread across Europe, and I will have to personally meet one of them and will have to convince him to carry out attack on the street of Paris, and then from there I'll proceed to "Yemen" and again meet the man of my own organization and will request him the plan an attack on the two ships in the Persian Gulf Sea.

Fazal queries, do you think that your man in "Paris" will agree to carry out snuck attack on the pedestrians, Waqar laughs, replies, why not? We have many fanatics, this fanatics have been severely brainwashed, in the name of religion they are willing to go to any extent, they happily takes lives of others and are more than happy to sacrifice their own life.

Fazal says, ok, than, you please get the ball rolling, and I shall move from here and go to "Dubai" from where I'll supervise the whole "terror operation," Waqar assures Fazal, you live it to me and I'll ensure the whole terror attacks are executed successfully.

Fazal gets up and hugs Waqar, show him thumbs up sign and concludes the meeting, Fazal departs from Somalia's "Al Noora jihadist camp" and travels back to Kenyan city of "Nairobi" from where he takes flight to "Dubai."

Waqar starts making his move, Waqar illegally but successfully hiding himself from the prying eyes of security forces reaches French city of "Paris."

Waqar contacts his "Al Noora group" member of the sleeping cell in Paris, Waqar meets a man whose name is "Abdulla Ahmad," Abdulla greets Waqar.

Waqar starts conversation with Abdulla, Waqar nobble Abdulla, he says, my friend with the grace of god today I've come to meet you and you will be proud of yourself that today god has send an opportunity for you, with beaming smile Abdulla ask, what my brother? Waqar elaborates, these infidels forces have once again started bitterly harassing our esteem community, the infidels army has in recent past inflicted major harm to our community, it's about time we take revenge with this infidels and teach them a lesson.

Abdulla Ahmad queries, please tell me, what I have to do? Waqar emotionally replies, the onus is on the shoulder of young people like you to save our community, which is in grave danger, the infidels are living no stone unturned to harm the interest of our community.

Abdulla's emotions run high, he vociferates, please tell me, what I've to do? My blood is boiling and I won't hesitate a bit in sacrificing my life for the cause of my religion, I won't to quench my thirst with the blood of these infidels, I want to take revenge with these infidels for the blood of my communities brothers and sisters who all have lost their lives.

Waqar stares into the eyes of desperate "Abdulla Ahmad" and says, my thoughts are with you, I'm profoundly happy to see the passion in you, your resolve to harm the infidels, Abdulla retorts, thank you "Sir" now tell me, what I have to do?

Waqar nods his head, says, ok, listen, on this Saturday afternoon, you'll have to carry a big sharp pointed knife with you and go to any of the "Parisian" street which is moderately crowded and there you have to run amok, and randomly whoever comes your way you see them you have to start to brutally attacking them with knife to the pedestrians present on the street, and ensure the pedestrians are severely wounded and even if they succumb to "death" its ok.

Abdulla agrees, yes, I'm ready to do this job, but, you tell me, what happens next? Once I brutally harm the pedestrians, after that, what am I supposed to do? Waqar emotionally kisses Abdulla on his forehead and comments, you are harming the infidels in god's name, hence you should not fear the consequences, Waqar add, after you are done with your attack on the pedestrians you have to loudly recite our religions sermons quotes form our holy book, and then you may live yourself to destiny.

Abdulla ask, what brother? Waqar says, once you have finished your job of attacking the infidels on the street, you can run away from the site, there's high probability that in doing so you may either get killed in police encounter or you may be arrested or you have an "option" if you want to avoid either of the thing happening to you, you may well kill your own self.

Abdulla Ahmad emotionally charges, commits to "Waqar Iqbal," he says, please don't worry "Sir" it's my commitment and pledge that I've devoted my life for my religion and I don't damn care about consequences, let me first kill the infidels than I'll decide myself as in what I have to do about myself.

Waqar compliments Abdulla for his courage and says, thank you, god bless you, Abdulla reassures Waqar, he says, the job of harming the pedestrians on the street will be done "full and final."

Waqar concludes the meeting with Abdulla Ahmad and now he's on his way to Yemen to meet his other colleagues of his own "Al Noora jihadist group."

Waqar reaches Yemen and goes to his "Al Noora jihadist" camp base in Yemen.

Waqar Iqbal meets his colleague Waleed, Waleed is a man in charge of "Al Noora jihadist group's" Yemeni region.

Waqar holds close door meeting with Waleed and explains to him that he has to organize a snuck terror attack on any two large ships "Tankers" which are loaded with oil and are sailing in the waters of Persian Gulf Sea and are on its way to their destination.

Waqar and Waleed together rack up there brain for well over four hours discussing the nitty-gritty of planning strategy of attacking and blasting the ships in the middle of the sea.

Finally they get the strategy ready, Waqar and Waleed concludes there meeting, they've evolve the right strategy of blasting the ships.

Waleed summons his henchmen "Abdel and Yusuf" to meet him, Waleed renders the responsibility of blasting the ships to "Yusuf," Waleed and Waqar tell Yusuf, you are the captain and it's you who have to spearhead the terror attack and carry out high intensity powerful bomb blast on the ships in the middle of Persian Sea, and to ensure the ships you attack gets obliterate completely.

Abdel and Yusuf assures "Waleed and Waqar" please don't worry we'll plan and execute the terror attack immaculately and there won't be any error, Waleed informs Yusuf to be ready to move with your team, Waleed tells Yusuf, prepare your jihadist men's and be ready to sail, set yourselves for the mission.

Yusuf and Abdel commits themselves and takes resolve to finish the job of blasting the ships.

Waqar contacts Fazal khan Bangash who is currently lodge himself in Five Star Hotel in Dubai, Waqar informs Fazal, everything is meticulously planned, we've evolve nice strategy to carry out terror attack in the waters of Persian Sea as well as on the street of Paris, Fazal happy to listen what Waqar informs him, he replies, excellent, go ahead, and terrorise the world, Waqar replies, confirm, we are ready to go.

Chapter 20

The day is Saturday, and after his afternoon prayers and after having lunch, Abdulla Ahmad gets ready to walk down the street, Abdulla gets his knife ready ensures the knife's blade is sharp enough, put the knife in his bag, and Abdulla Ahmad like a true jihadist steps out of his apartment and goes on his mission, Abdulla reaches the busy street in Paris, he looks around, Abdulla loud shout in the name of god and he runs amok and starts randomly attacking the pedestrians on the street complete chaotic scence is being played on, the crowds starts running helter shelter and Abdulla busy stabbing and wounding people whoever he spots or whoever comes his way, after brutally stabbing and severely wounding nearly dozen plus innocent people on the street Abdulla starts reciting religious sermons and tries to flee from the site of the incident, the police chases him, and Abdulla is killed defying his arrest, the bullet from the revolver of the local cop kills Abdulla Ahmad.

The terror attack on the street of Paris evokes strong condemnation from all section of society and international community as well condemn the terror attack on the street of Paris, the whole country and international community mourns the deaths of few of the wounded pedestrians who lost their lives, after receiving severe injuries from the knife of Abdulla Ahmad.

One part of Fazal's terror deal is completed in Paris, and now Fazal's eyes is set on the next big terror attack which is above to happen in the Persian Sea "The Blasting of Ships."

Fazal also an astute businessman, he knows well that blasting of large oil "vessels" (ships) in the Persian Region will have its ripple effect on international economy and on crude oil prices in international market, Fazal makes a wise move to make additional money, (others misery is my earning opportunity) Fazal with help of his friends an financial consultant, Fazal places his bets on in the commodity derivatives market and he takes position in the crude oil derivatives "Call and Put Options."

The day is Monday, and Yusuf and Abdel the two men belonging to "Al Noora jihadist group" are sailing in the waters of Persian Sea in two separate speedboat, Yusuf and Abdel are accompanied four jihadist each, there speed boat is loaded with high inflammable explosives materials, Yusuf and Abdel part ways and goes separate way searching for their targets.

Abdel delivers the first fatal blow, Abdel is the first to spot a large Ship vessel sailing in the waters of Persian Gulf Sea and moving towards Arabian Sea, Abdel encircle to large ship loaded with crude oil, Abdel tells his colleagues to throw explosive on the ship and blast the vessel.

Abdel colleagues the jihadist follows there captains instruction and blast the huge ship, Abdel steering the speedboat tries to save himself and his colleagues makes a quick turn of his speedboat and Abdel is a champion, he and his colleagues survives, they manage to make a quick escape from the site, the ship which they blast is totally decimated.

Yusuf as well spots a large Ship vessel carry crude oil to the country of its origin, Yusuf orders his subordinate colleagues to throw the explosives on the ship and blast it, the jihadist follows instruction of their commander "Yusuf," they throw the explosive on the large ship, Yusuf steering the speedboat also makes a valiant effort to save himself and his colleagues from the flames emanating from the ship which is on fire, but, No, Yusuf and his associates aren't as fortunate as there other colleagues Abdel and his associates, while trying to flee from the site, Yusuf's boat sinks in the sea, Yusuf as well as the members accompanying him are killed as well.

The blast of two major ship in the Persian Gulf Sea send tremor across the globe, stock indices plunges, oil prices rises, the international community is shell shocked, wide spread condemnation of terror attacks form every countries heads of states.

Frenetic phone calls are being made, the entire world is in shock, they fear may be the worse isn't over, and some more terror attacks may occur, major intelligence failure.

Fazal khan Bangash has successfully outwitted the mighty and powerful governments and there intelligence agencies.

Fazal Khan Bangash lodge in Dubai, he receives his payment that was promised to him from the mysterious organization, Fazal makes payments to his friend and "Al Noora jihadist" group chief Waqar Iqbal." Fazal has also made huge amount of money betting on crude oil derivatives in the commodity exchange.

Fazal makes his move, he takes flight out of Dubai and reaches his hometown Kabul in Afghanistan, Fazal Khan Bangash is back home back with his family, Fazal returns home triumphant.

Two gruesome incident of Terror Attack in quick succession "first on the street of Paris and second the blasting of two ships in the middle of Persian Sea" has rattle the international community, The Political fraternity as well as security agencies are baffle after the terror incidents.

Fazal back home overwhelmingly tired and outrageously concern, encumbered with thoughts of fear and anxiety, wondering what if the long hands "Law" reaches and grab my collar and punishes me the heinous crime I have committed of conniving with and helping the mysterious organization with carry out terror attack.

Fazal request both his wives "Yalda and Hala" to live him alone, Fazal confine himself in one room of his house and ponders as in what to do next.

One morning Fazal lives his home early morning and drives his vehicle to an unknown destination in wilderness.

Chapter 21

Fazal Khan Bangash reaches at the peak of the mountain, at a high altitude landscape, in pristine environment, Fazal sits on the mountains rock and vividly thinks.

"Sometimes you just need a Break in a Beautiful Place, Alone, to Figure Everything Out."

Past Success Become Best Practise, Best Practise Become Best Template, Best Template Becomes Unquestionable Sacred Truth.

Islam is the most misunderstood religion, The follower of Islam those who support Islam and its founder, have misunderstood and misconstrued it.

Even the opponent and bitter critic of Islam those who hate Islam and its founder, have misunderstood and have misconstrued Islam.

People as far back as history goes it seems, People waste pivotal moment of their life "thinking about god, talking about god, discussing about god, taking name of god as many time as they could during course of their life."

People invest so much of their valuable time in god and for god that this people tend to forget to understand themselves and develop falls beliefs and misconception about themselves.

After spending several hours in isolation away from home, wandering alone on the craggy mountains, Fazal heads back home.

Fazal reaches his home, he calls both his wives close to him, Fazal tells his wives "Yalda and Hala" it's time to go it's time to move on, Yalda ask, ok, but, where do we all go? Fazal replies, away from our hometown, far away from our people and never to return back to this insular society.

Fazal's second wife "Hala" ask, my dear husband, what's wrong with you today? What are you saying? Please be more perspicuous, Fazal says, please start packing bags, we have to live our motherland Afghanistan for good, we have to go and settle down in Australia and be there with our other family members who are already there.

Yalda and Hala jubilant to hear that they will no longer be staying in the most perilous country in the world "Afghanistan" starts packing bags and other stuff that they can carry along with them.

Fazal loaded with cash, Fazal has earned "Millions of US Dollars," Fazal is hugely a rich man.

Fazal Khan Bangash bids final adieu to his beloved country "Afghanistan and his hometown Kabul" and along with his two wives and daughter "Nagma" and stepdaughter/stepsister "Heena," flies out of Afghanistan and goes to Australia for good.

Fazal with his own immediate family reaches Australian city of "Perth," and he joins his mother "Farida" and his sisters "Firdoz and Zarine" and his elder brother "Karmal."

Fazal's mother and sisters are ecstatic to see Fazal and his wives in Australia and are overwhelm by the fact that they will all be staying together in a peaceful country like Australia.

In free liberal and modern country like Australia, Fazal family as well have got accustomed to the new modern and liberal culture.

Fazal's wives "Yalda and Hala" particularly thanks him, as both this women "Yalda and Hala" were hard pressed at one point in their lives, Fazal played crucial role in lifting his family's fortune.

Fazal's second wife "Hala" gives birth to his second child, Hala gives birth to a "Son" and Fazal first wife becomes pregnant again for the second time.

This is the most propitious moment of "Fazal's" life, Fazal starts his new business in Australia, Fazal buys a Hotel in "Perth" and he also buys couple of guess, what? He buys couple of cargo ships and starts shipping company.

Fazal's overall observation and his concluding remark is,

EACH INDIVIDUAL HUMAN'S BRAIN HAS GOT TWO SIDE OF IT, THE RIGHT SIDE AND THE LEFT SIDE, HAVE A LISTEN, THE LEFT SIDE

HAS GOT NOTHING RIGHT ABOUT IT, THE RIGHT SIDE HAS GOT NOTHING RIGHT ABOUT IT

www.ingramcontent.com/pod-product-compliance
Lightning Source LLC
LaVergne TN
LVHW080815170826
845678LV00011B/2022